Light Ahead
for the Negro

Light Ahead for the Negro

Edward A. Johnson

MINT EDITIONS

Light Ahead for the Negro was first published in 1904.

This edition published by Mint Editions 2021.

ISBN 9781513296838 | E-ISBN 9781513298337

Published by Mint Editions®

 MINT
EDITIONS

minteditionbooks.com

Publishing Director: Jennifer Newens
Design & Production: Rachel Lopez Metzger
Project Manager: Micaela Clark
Typesetting: Westchester Publishing Services

CONTENTS

I

The Lost Airship—Unconsciousness

From my youth up I had been impressed with the idea of working among the Negroes of the Southern states. My father was an abolitionist before the war and afterward an ardent supporter of missionary efforts in the South, and his children naturally imbibed his spirit of readiness and willingness at all times to assist the cause of the freedmen.

I concluded in the early years of my young manhood that I could render the Negroes no greater service than by spending my life in their midst, helping to fit them for the new citizenship that had developed as a result of the war. My mind was made up throughout my college course at Yale; and, while I did not disclose my purpose, I resolved to go South as soon as I was through college and commence my chosen life-work. In keeping with this design, I kept posted on every phase of the so-called "Negro problem"; I made it my constant study. When I had finished college I made application to the Union Missionary Association for a position as teacher in one of their Negro schools in a town in Georgia, and after the usual preliminaries I received my certificate of appointment.

It was June, 1906, the year that dirigible airships first came into actual use, after the innumerable efforts of scores of inventors to solve final problems, which for a long time seemed insurmountable. Up to this time the automobile—now relegated to commercial uses, or, like the bicycle, to the poorer classes—had been the favored toy of the rich, and it was thought that the now common one hundred and one hundred and fifty horse-power machines were something wonderful and that their speed—a snail's pace, compared with the airship—was terrific. It will be remembered that inside of a few months after the first really successful airships appeared a wealthy man in society could hardly have hoped to retain his standing in the community without owning one, or at least proving that he had placed an order for one with a fashionable foreign manufacturer, so great was the craze for them, and so widespread was the industry—thanks to the misfortune of the poor devil who solved the problem and neglected to protect his rights thoroughly. Through this fatal blunder on his part, their manufacture and their use became world-wide, almost at once, in spite of countless legal attempts to limit the production, in order to keep up the cost.

A wealthy friend of mine had a ship of the finest Parisian make, the American machines still being unfashionable, in which we had often made trips together and which he ran himself. As I was ready to go to my field of labor, he invited me to go with him to spend from Saturday to Sunday in the City of Mexico, which I had never seen, and I accepted.

We started, as usual, from the new aërial pier at the foot of West Fifty-ninth Street, New York City, then one of the wonders of the world, about one o'clock, in the midst of a cloud of machines bound for country places in different parts of the United States and we were peacefully seated after dinner, enjoying the always exhilarating sensation of being suspended in space without support—for my friend had drawn the covering from the floor of clear glass in the car, which was coming into use in some of the new machines—when there was a terrific report. The motor had exploded!

We looked at each other in horror. This indeed was what made air-travelling far-and-away the most exciting of sports. Human beings had not yet come to regard with indifference accidents which occurred in mid-air.

My friend picked his way through a tangled mass of machinery to the instruments. We were rising rapidly and the apparatus for opening the valve of the balloon was broken. Without saying a word, he started to climb up the tangle of wire ropes to the valve itself; a very dangerous proceeding, because many of the ropes were loosened from their fastenings. We suddenly encountered a current of air that changed our course directly east. (We had been steering south and had gone about six hundred miles.) It drew us up higher and higher. I glanced through the floor but the earth was almost indistinguishable, and was disappearing rapidly. There was absolutely nothing that I could do. I looked up again at my friend, who was clambering up rather clumsily, I remember thinking at the moment. The tangle of ropes and wires looked like a great grape vine. Just then the big ship gave a lurch. He slipped and pitched forward, holding on by one hand. Involuntarily, I closed my eyes for a moment. When I opened them again, *he was gone*!

My feelings were indescribable. I commenced to lose consciousness, owing to the altitude and the ship was ascending more rapidly every moment.

Finally I became as one dead.

II

To Earth Again—One Hundred Years Later

O ne day an archaic-looking flying machine, a curiosity, settled from aërial heights on to the lawn of one Dr. Newell, of Phœnix, Georgia.

When found I was unconscious and even after I had revived I could tell nothing of my whereabouts, as to whither I was going, or whence I had come; I was simply there, "a stranger in a strange land," without being able to account for anything.

I noticed however that the people were not those I had formerly left or that I expected to see. I was bewildered—my brain was in a whirl—I lapsed again into a trance-like state.

When I regained my full consciousness I found myself comfortably ensconced in a bed in an airy room apparently in the home of some well-to-do person. The furniture and decorations in the room were of a fashion I had never seen before, and the odd-looking books in the bookcase near the bed were written by authors whose names I did not know. I seemed to have awakened from a dream, a dream that had gone from me, but that had changed my life.

Looking around in the room, I found that I was the only occupant. I resolved to get up and test the matter. I might still be dreaming. I arose, dressed myself—my suit case lay on a table, just as I had packed it—and hurriedly went downstairs, wondering if I were a somnambulist and thinking I had better be careful lest I fall and injure myself. I heard voices and attempted to speak and found my voice unlike any of those I heard in the house. I was just passing out of the front door, intending to walk around on the large veranda that extended on both sides of the house, when I came face to face with a very attractive young lady who I subsequently learned was the niece of my host and an expert trained nurse. She had taken charge of me ever since my unexpected arrival on her uncle's lawn.

She explained that she had been nursing me and seemed very much mortified that I should have come to consciousness at a moment when she was not present, and have gotten out of the room and downstairs before she knew it. I could see chagrin in her countenance and to reassure her I said, "You needn't worry about your bird's leaving the cage, he shall not fly away, for in the first place he is quite unable to, and in the second place why should he flee from congenial company?"

"I am glad you are growing better," she said, "and I am sure we are all very much interested in your speedy recovery, Mr.—What shall I call you?" she said hesitatingly.

I attempted to tell her my name, but I could get no further than, "My name is—" I did not know my own name!

She saw my embarrassment and said, "O, never mind the name, I'll let you be my anonymous friend. Tell me where you got that very old flying machine?"

Of course I knew, but I could not tell her. My memory on this point had failed me also. She then remarked further that papers found in my pocket indicated that a Mr. Gilbert Twitchell had been appointed to a position as teacher in a Missionary School in the town of Ebenezer, Georgia, in the year 1906, and inquired if these "old papers" would help me in locating my friends. She left me for a moment and returned with several papers, a diary and a large envelope containing a certificate of appointment to said school.

She stated that inquiry had already been made and that "old records" showed that a person by the name of Twitchell had been appointed in 1906, according to the reading of the certificate, and that while *en route* to his prospective field of labor in an air-ship he was supposed to have come to an untimely death, as nothing had been seen or heard of him since. Further than that the official records did not go.

"Now, we should be very glad to have you tell us how you came by that certificate," she suggested.

I was aghast. I was afraid to talk to her or to look about me. And the more fully I came to myself the more I felt that I did not dare to ask a question. The shock of one answer might kill me.

I summoned all my strength, and spoke hurriedly, more to prevent her speaking again than to say anything.

"Perhaps I can tell you something later on," I said hoarsely. "I find my memory quite cloudy, in fact, I seem to be dreaming."

She saw my misery and suggested that I go into "the room used to cure nervousness" and that I remain as long as possible. I passed stupidly through the door she held open for me and had hardly sat down before I felt soothed. The only color visible was violet,—walls, ceiling, furniture, carpet, all violet of different shades. An artificial light of the same color filled the room. And the air!—What was there in it?

A desk was at the other end of the large apartment. As my eyes roved about the strange looking place I saw on it an ordinary calendar pad, the only thing in the room that closely resembled objects I had seen before. The moment that I realized what it was I felt as though I was about to have a nervous chill. I dared not look at it, even from that distance. But the delicious air, the strength-giving light revived me in spite of myself. For full five minutes I sat there, staring, before starting over to look at it; for though I knew not who I was, and though I had passed through only two rooms of the house, and had met only one person, I had divined the truth a thousand times.

As I slowly neared it I saw the day of the month, the twenty-fourth. Nearer and nearer I came, finally closing my eyes as the date of the year in the corner became *almost* legible—just as I had done in the car of the air-ship, that awful moment. I moved a little nearer. I could read it now! I opened my eyes and glanced, then wildly tore the pads apart, to see if they were all alike—and fell to the floor once more.

It was the year *two thousand and six*, just one hundred years from the date of my appointment to the position of a teacher in the South!

IN A SHORT TIME I regained complete consciousness, and under the influence of that wonderful room became almost myself again. I learned that I had not really been left alone but had been observed, through a device for that purpose, by both the doctor and his niece, and on her return I related my whole story to her as far as I could then remember it.

The strangest and most unaccountable part was that though I had been away from the earth about one hundred years, yet, here I was back again still a young man, showing no traces of age and I had lived a hundred years. This was afterward accounted for by the theory that at certain aerial heights the atmosphere is of such a character that no physical changes take place in bodies permitted to enter it.

The physical wants of my body seemed to have been suspended, and animation arrested until the zone of atmosphere immediately surrounding the earth was reached again, when gradually life and consciousness returned.

I have no recollection of anything that transpired after I lost consciousness and the most I can say of it all is that the experience was that of one going to sleep at one end of his journey and waking up at his destination.

III

At the Public Library with Irene

The next time I met my nurse was by chance. I saw her at the public library near Dr. Newell's house, where I often went to sit and think the first few days after my rebirth into the world. She had left the Newell residence on the night of the day she had put me in the violet room, being called to some special duty elsewhere. I approached her with a kindly salutation which she reciprocated in a manner indicating that she was pleased to meet me. In the meantime I had found out her name—Irene Davis—and had also found out that an elective course in a training school for scientific nursing was according to the custom of the times, which regarded such a course as indispensable to the education of a liberally trained young woman.

Our conversation drifted along as to my personal comforts until I told her that I had heard that I was to be called upon to deliver a written account of my recollections of the past, especially in reference to the Negro question.

"I suppose Dr. Newell is at the bottom of that," she remarked, "he is so intensely interested in the Negro question that he would be the first one to make the suggestion. I really believe that he refused to allow you to be taken to the City Hospital when you were found on his lawn because he almost divined that you might have a message from another age for him on that subject. The city authorities yielded to his wishes and assigned me to assist in caring for you at his residence, instead of at the hospital.

"I found very little to do, however, but would like to recall to you the beneficial effects of the violet room, which I see had the desired results. It always does, and many people who can afford it, especially physicians, are now installing these rooms in their houses for the benefit of neurotic patients, on whom the violet rays of electricity, coupled with neurium, a newly discovered chemical preparation, similar to radium, has a most remarkable effect."

I remarked that I had taken no medicine and really felt better than ever in either of my lives. "Well," said she, laughing, "I trust you may be able to recall all about the past and give a most excellent account of it in your paper for the Bureau of Public Utility—and don't fail to send me a copy!"

"Are you at all interested in the question," I asked.

"All Southerners are interested in that question. I am a teacher in a Sunday School for Negro children and a member of a Young Ladies' Guild which was organized expressly for reaching Negro children that may need help. We visit the families and talk with the parents, impress on them ideas of economy, direct them in caring for the sick, and instruct them in the most scientific methods of sanitation. I am really fond of these people and the happiest moments of my life are spent with them—they are of a different temperament from us, so mild and good natured,—so complacent and happy in their religious worship and their music is simply enchanting!—Don't you like to hear them sing, Mr. Twitchell?"

I remarked that I was very fond of their singing, and that I had been delighted with a visit I had recently made to the Dvorak Conservatory, where the Negro's musical talent seemed to have been miraculously developed.

I further remarked, to myself, "How congenial in tastes and sympathy we seem to be, and how beautiful you are!" She moved me strangely as she stood there with her black hair, rosy cheeks, large good-natured black eyes, her Venus-like poise of neck and shoulders, and a mouth neither large nor small but full of expression, and showing a wealth of pearls when she laughed—and all this coupled with such noble aspirations, and such deep womanly sympathy.

I said to her, "Miss Davis, I am certainly glad to learn that our sentiments on the Negro question coincide so thoroughly and if any encouragement were needed, I should certainly feel like offering it, as a stimulus in your efforts."

"All humanity needs encouragement," she replied, "and I am human; and so are these people around us who are of a different race. They need encouragement and in my humble way I hope to be of some service to them. Their chances have not been as favorable as ours, but they have been faithful and true with the talents they have."

"So I understand you are assisting in this work more from a sense of duty than as a diversion?" I observed.

"Yes, that is true," she said, "but nevertheless I really get considerable recreation in it. I find these people worthy of assistance and competent to fill many places that they otherwise could not but for the help of our Guild."

"So you have found that success does not always come to the worthy," I suggested, "if those who are worthy have no outside influence? I can remember people who worked hard all their lives for promotion and who not only did not get it, but often witnessed others less skilled and deserving than themselves pushed forward ahead of them. This was especially true of the Negro race in my time. The Negroes were told that Negro ability would sell for as much in the market as white, but while this was encouraging in some respects and true in many cases, it could by no means be laid down as a rule."

"I agree with you," she said, "in part; for the feeling no doubt prevails among some people that the lines of cleavage should move us naturally to do more for our own than for a different race, and that spirit occasionally crops out, but the spirit of helpfulness to Negroes has now become so popular that it permeates all classes and there is practically no opposition to them."

"You are a long way removed from the South of the past," said I, "where to have done such work as you are engaged in would have disgraced you, and have branded you for social ostracism."

She replied that there was no criticism at all for engaging in such work but only for doing more for one race than another.

"You Georgians had degenerated in my day," I remarked. "The Southern colonies under such men as Oglethorpe seemed to have higher ideals than had their descendants of later times. Oglethorpe was opposed to slavery and refused to allow it in the Colony of Georgia while he was governor; he was also a friend to the Indians and to Whitfield in his benevolent schemes, but the Georgian of my day was a different character altogether from the Oglethorpe type. He justified slavery and burned Negroes at the stake, and the 'Cracker class' were a long ways removed from the Oglethorpe type of citizenship, both in appearance and intelligence. I notice, too, Miss Davis, that you never use the words 'colored people' but say 'Negro,' instead."

"That is because these people themselves prefer to be called Negroes. They are proud of the term Negro and feel that you are compromising if you refer to them as 'colored people.'"

"That is quite a change, too," said I, "from the past; for in my time the race did not like the term Negro so well because it sounded so much like 'nigger,' which was a term of derision. I notice that this term also has become obsolete with you—another sign of progress. In fact, I fear that the ideas I had in 1906, when I started on my trip to work as a missionary among the Negroes, would be laughed at now, so far have you progressed beyond me. Indeed, I am quite confused at times in trying to conform to my new conditions."

At this juncture she suggested that she had almost broken an engagement by chatting with me so long, and would have to hurry off to meet it. In taking her departure she remarked that perhaps it was worth while to break an engagement to talk with one who had had so unusual an experience. "I may be quite an unusual character," said I, "but probably too ancient to be of interest to so modern a person as yourself."

She did not reply to this, but left with a smile and a roguish twinkle in her eye.

I found on inquiry at the library that Negroes in the South were now allowed the use of the books, and that they were encouraged to read by various prizes, offered especially for those who could give the best written analyses of certain books which were suggested by the library committee.

IV

NOW AND THEN

I had scarcely recovered my equilibrium and become able to give an account of myself before I was formally called on by the "Chief of the Bureau of Public Utility" of the country to make a statement about the Negro problem in my time, Dr. Newell having informed him that I was interested in that subject.

Here follows the substance of what I wrote as I read it over to Dr. Newell before sending it:

"Many changes considered well nigh impossible one hundred years ago have taken place in almost all phases of the so-called Negro problem. One of the most noticeable instances to me is the absence of slurs at individual Negroes and at the race as a whole in your newspapers. Such headlines as 'Another Coon Caught,' 'The Burly Black Brute Foiled,' 'A Ham Colored Nigger in the Hen House' and 'This Coon Wants to be Called Mister,' are, to me, conspicuous by their absence. In the old days, in referring to a Negro who had made a speech of some merit he was called 'Professor,' but in making a reference to him as being connected with politics the same person was dubbed 'Jim' or 'Tom.' Fights between three white men and two Negroes were published, under glaring headlines, as 'Race Riots.' The usual custom of dealing out the vices of the Negro race as a morning sensation in the daily papers evidently fell into 'innocuous desuetude,' and the daily papers having dropped the custom, the weeklies, which were merely echoes of the dailies, also left off the habit, so that now neither the city people nor farmers have their prejudices daily and weekly inflamed by exaggerated portrayals of the Negroes' shortcomings.

"The character of no individual and in fact of no race can long endure in America when under the persistent fire of its newspapers. Newspapers mould public opinion. Your organization for the dissemination of news has it in its power to either kill or make alive in this respect. Our organization, called the News Distributing Bureau, was formerly in the hands of people whose policy designedly necessitated the portrayal of the Negro in his worst light before the people, in order that certain schemes against the race might be fostered, and seemed to take special delight in publishing every mean act of every bad Negro, and leaving unrecorded the thousands of credible acts of the good ones.

"Like Lincoln's emancipation proclamation, this wholesale assassination of Negro character in the newspapers was strictly a political 'war measure,' intended for political use only. Its design was to prejudice the race in the eyes of the world and thus enable the white supremacy advocates, North and South, to perfect the political annihilation of the Negro. The Negro farmer knew little about what was going on; he was making corn and cotton, and to tell him in public assemblies would be considered 'incendiary,' and 'stirring up strife between the races,' and the individual who might be thus charged would certainly have to leave 'between two suns,' as the phrase was. However, the general desire among leading Negroes was for peace at any sacrifice, and they studiously labored to that end. The South ought to have thanked the Negro preachers and the Negro school teachers for the reign of peace in that section, because it was due almost wholly to their efforts.

"Then, too, the public schools, which were at that period the boast of the South, in support of her contention of friendliness to the Negro, served the purpose of quieting many a Negro who might otherwise have been disposed to 'talk too much.'[1] Be it remembered that at this time it was considered virtually a social crime to employ a Negro as a clerk in a store or elsewhere. This feeling extended from Delaware to Texas, and the thousands of Negroes who were coming out of the various public schools, and the institutions for higher training established by Northern philanthropists, had practically no calling open to them, as educated men and women, save that of teaching. The door of hope was shut in their face and they were censured for not doing better under such impossible handicaps. It was like closing the stable door and whipping the horse for not going in! A few entered the professions of law, pharmacy and medicine, some engaged in business, but no great number for the following reasons:

"First—In the professions the white professional man was by habit and custom very generally employed by the colored people, while the colored professional man, by the conventional laws of society, was rarely or never employed by white people.

---

1. The white supremacy people accomplished this by employing them as teachers. If they continued to talk too much, they lost their jobs.

"Second—The natural disposition of the colored people to patronize white merchants and professional men in preference to their own was a factor to be reckoned with in looking for the *causas rerum*—a kind of one-sided arrangement whereby the whites got the Negroes' money but the Negroes could not get theirs—in the professions. In many of the small lines of business, however, the Negro was patronized by the whites.

"So that—with the News Bureau making capital every morning of the corruption in the race; with the efforts of Southern ministers who had taken charge of Northern pulpits, to strew seeds of poison by proclaiming, on the commission of every offense by a Negro, 'We told you that the Negro was not worth the freedom you gave him,' 'We told you he wasn't fit for citizenship and that the money you have spent for his education is worse than wasted;' with the constant assertions that his only place is 'behind a mule,' that education made him a greater criminal, that 'the Southern people are his best friends' because 'we overlook his follies' and 'treat him kindly if he will stay in his place;' with the money interests clamoring for the South 'to be let alone' with the Negro question, for fear of unsettling business and causing a slump in Southern securities; with the claims that, to keep the railroads earning dividends, to keep the cotton market active, the Negro must be handled according to the serfdom or shotgun plan, and that the best task master so far found was the Southern white man, who had proven himself wonderfully adept in getting good crops from Negro labor—with these and many other excuses, the question of raising the Negro in the scale of civilization was left to posterity.

"'What is he worth to us now?' That is the only question with which we are concerned, was the ruling thought, if not the open confession.

"Let it be understood that statistics (which the Negro did not compile) showed that the race at that time was, as a mass, the most illiterate, the least thrifty, and the most shiftless and criminal of any class of American citizens—dividing the population into natives—Irish emigrants, German emigrants, Italians, Jews, and Poles. This was a fact that hurt, regardless of who was responsible for it.

"Then the question of color cut no small figure in this problem. The Negro's color classified him; it rang the signal bell for drawing 'the color line' as soon as he was seen, and it designated and pointed him out as a marked man, belonging to that horrible criminal class whose revolting deeds were revealed every day in the newspapers. No wonder he was shunned, no wonder the children and women were afraid of

EDWARD A. JOHNSON

him! The great mass of the people took the newspaper reports as true. They never read between the lines and seldom read the corrections of errors[2] that had been made. In some cases the first report had been that a Negro had committed a crime, and later it was discovered that a white man with his face blacked had been the perpetrator. Some one has said, 'Let me write the songs of a people and I will control their religious sentiments.' In a country like America where the newspapers are so plentiful and where people rely on them so implicitly, those who control the newspapers may be said to control the views of the people on almost any public question. With 30 per cent of the Negro population illiterate, with a criminal record double that of any of the emigrant classes above outlined, with the News Distributing Bureau against it, with no political or social standing—pariahs in the land— with Northern capital endorsing serfdom, with their inability to lose their race identity, on account of their color—we realize how heavy the odds were against the Negro race at that time.

"As a Negro orator once put it, 'De Southern white man's on top'er de nigger and de Yankee white man's on top er de Southern white man and de bad nigger's on top er dem bofe!'

"I now come to some of the proposed solutions of the problem. Various meetings were held all over the country to discuss the Negro problem, and many a mediocre white man who thirsted for a little newspaper notoriety, or political preferment, in both the North and the South, had his appetite in this direction satisfied by writing or saying something on the Negro question. One Thomas Dixon tried to out Herod Herod in taking up the exceptional cases of Negro criminality and using them in an attempt to convince his readers of the Negro's unfitness for citizenship. A public speaker named John Temple Graves[3] made lecture tours advocating deportation as the only solution of the

---

2. "Errors" like the following, for instance: "A special dispatch from Charleston, S. C., to the Atlanta Journal, reads: 'While dying in Colleton county, former Section Foreman Jones, of the Atlantic Coast Line Road, has confessed being the murderer of his wife at Ravenel, S. C., fourteen miles from Charleston, in May, 1902, for which crime three Negroes were lynched. The crime which was charged to the Negroes was one of the most brutal ever committed in this State, and after the capture of the Negroes quick work was made of them by the mob.'

"Comment is certainly superfluous. What must be the feelings of those who participated in the lynching." (*Raleigh, N. C., Morning Post.*)

3. The following were the views of Mr. Noah W. Cooper, a Nashville lawyer, on one of Mr. Graves' addresses:

problem, rejecting as unsound the theories of Booker Washington, who was advocating industrial education as the main factor in solving the problem, because of the consequent clash that would arise between

---

"John Temple Graves' address in Chicago contains more errors and inconsistencies about the so-called Negro problem than any recent utterance on the subject.

"He says that God has established the 'metes and bounds' of the Negro's habitation, but he never pointed out a single mete nor a single bound. He says, 'Let us put the Negro kindly and humanely out of the way;' but his vision again faded and he never told us where to put the darkey.

"If Mr. Graves' inspiration had not been as short as a clam's ear and he had gone on and given us the particular spot on the globe to which we should 'kindly and humanely' kick the darkey 'out of the way,' then we might have asked, who will take the darkey's place in the South? Who will plow and hoe and pick out 12,000,000 bales of cotton? Who will sing in the rice fields? Who will raise the sugar cane? Who will make our 'lasses and syrup? Who will box and dip our turpentine? Who will cut and saw the logs, and on his body bear away the planks from our thousands of sawmills? Who will get down into the mud and swamps and build railroads for rich contractors? Who will work out their lives in our phosphate mines and factories, and in iron and coal mines? Who will be roustabouts on our rivers and on our wharves to be conscripted when too hot for whites to work? Who will fill the darkey's place in the Southern home?

"Oh, I suppose Mr. Graves would say, we will get Dutch and Poles, and Hungarians, Swedes or other foreigners; or we will ourselves do all the work of the Negro. To me this is neither possible nor desirable.

"The South don't want to kick the Negro out, as I understand it. The separation of the Negro from us now—his exile, *nolens volens*—would be a greater calamity to us than his emancipation or his enfranchisement ever has been. We need him and he needs us.

"Mr. Graves says that God never did intend that 'opposite and antagonistic races should live together.'

"That seems to me to be as wild as to say that God intended all dogs to stay on one island; all sheep on another; all lions on another; or to say that all corn should grow in America and all wheat in Russia.

"Mr. Graves cites no 'thus saith the Lord' to back up his new revelation that antagonistic races must live separated.

"What God is it whose mind Mr. Graves is thus revealing? Surely it can't be the God of the Bible—for He allowed the Jews to live 400 years among the Egyptians; then over 500 years in and out of captivity among the Canaanites; then in captivity nearly 100 years in Babylon; then under the Romans; then sold by the Romans; and from then to now the Jews—the most separate and exclusive of peoples—God's chosen people of the Old Covenant—they have lived anywhere, among all people. Surely Mr. Graves is not revealing the mind of the God to whom the original thirteen colonies bowed down in prayer; the God of the Declaration of Independence and the God of George Washington and Thomas Jefferson. For how many different races were planted in this new world? English, Dutch, Swedes, Quakers, Puritans, Catholics, French Huguenots, the poor, the rich—more antagonism than you can find between 'Buckra' and the 'nigger.' Yet all these antagonisms, such as they were, did not prevent our forefathers from uniting in one country, under one flag, in the common desire for political freedom, moral intelligence and individual nobility of character.

EDWARD A. JOHNSON

white and colored mechanics—rejecting also as unsound the theory of higher education; because that would develop in the Negro a longing for equality which the white man would not give and was never known

"Under Mr. Graves' God every colony would have become a petty nation, with a Chinese wall around it. Mr. Graves' inconsistencies reached a climax when he said in one breath, 'I appeal for the imperial destiny of our mighty race,' and then in the next breath says, 'let us put the Negro out.' Is it any more imperial to boss the Filipino abroad than it is to boss the Negro at home?

"The God of the Bible commands peace among races and nations, not war; friendship, not antagonism and hatred. Did not Paul, a Jew, become a messenger to the Gentiles? Did he not write the greater part of the New Testament of Christianity while living in Gentile and pagan Rome? Did not Christ set example to the world when He, a Jew, at Jacob's well, preached His most beautiful sermon to a poor Samaritan woman? Winding up that great sermon by telling the woman and the world that not the place of his abode and worship, but the good character of man—'in spirit and in truth'—was the only true worship. And that is the only exclusive place whose metes and bounds God has set for any man to live, 'in spirit and in truth.'

"How idle to talk of shutting off each race, as it were, into pens like pigs to fatten them. This penning process will neither fatten their bodies, enlighten their minds nor ennoble their souls. Can Mr. Graves tell us how much good the great Chinese wall has done for man? If he can, he can tell us how much good will come to us by putting the darkey out, and locking the door. Mr. Graves' idea would reverse all the maxims of Christianity. It would be much better for Mr. Graves' idea of the separation of antagonisms to be applied to different classes of occupations, of persons that are antagonistic. For instance, the dram-seller is antagonistic to all homes and boys and girls; therefore, put all dram-sellers and dram-shops on one island, and all the homes and boys and girls on another island, far, far away! Now there is your idea, Mr. Graves! Then, again, all horse thieves, bank breakers, train robbers, forgers, counterfeiters are antagonistic to honest men; so here, we will put them all in the District of Columbia and all the honest men in Ohio, and build a high wall between. All the bad boys we would put in a pen; and all us good boys, we will go to the park and have a picnic and laugh at the nincompoop bad boys whose destiny we have penned up! Ah, Mr. Graves could no more teach us this error than could he reverse the decree of Christ to let the wheat and tares grow together until harvest. The seclusion or isolation of an individual or a race is not the road that God has blazed out for the highest attainments. The Levite of the great parable drew his robes close about him and 'passed by on the other side'—like Mr. Graves would have us do the Negro, except that instead of passing him by we would 'put him behind us'—a mere difference of words. But the good Samaritan got down and nursed the dirty, wounded bleeding Jew; sacrificed his time and money to heal his wounds. Now that Levite must be Mr. Graves' ideal Southerner! He says the Negro is an unwilling, blameless, unwholesome, unwelcome element. So was the robbed and bleeding Jew to the Levite; but did that excuse the Levite's wrong? Ought the Levite to have put the groaning man 'out of the way' of his 'imperial destiny' by kicking him out of the road?

"Nay, verily. By the time that Mr. Graves gets all of the antagonistic races and all the antagonistic occupations and people of the world cornered off and fenced up in their God-prescribed 'metes and bounds,' and fences them each up, with stakes and riders to hold them in—by that time I am sure he will envy the job of Sysiphus. But there is a grain of sober truth in one thing Mr. Graves says—that the Negro is blameless."

to give an inferior race, a statement which all honest white people must regard as a base slander upon their Christianity.

"Bishop Turner, senior bishop of the African Methodist-Episcopal Church, one of the leading organizations of the Negro race, also advocated emigration to Africa as the only solution of the problem, on the grounds that the white people would never treat the Negro justly and that history furnished no instance where a slave race had ever become absolutely free in the land of its former owners, instancing that to be free the Jews had to leave Egypt; that William the Conqueror and his followers slaughtered the native Britons, rather than attempt to carry out what seemed to them an impossible task, that of teaching two races, a conquered race and a conquering one, to live side by side in peace.

"One Professor Bassett made enemies of the Southern newspapers and politicians by proposing *justice* and *equality* as a solution of the problem. The 'most unkindest cut of all' of Professor Bassett's saying was that Booker Washington was 'the greatest man, save Robert E. Lee, that the South had produced in a hundred years.' The politicians and their sympathizers seized upon this statement as being a good opportunity to keep up the discussion of the Negro issue, which many better disposed people were hoping would be dropped, according to promise, as soon as the Negroes had been deprived of the ballot by the amendments then being added to the constitutions of the Southern States. They rolled it over as a sweet morsel under their tongues. 'Othello's occupation,' they realized, would be gone without the 'nigger in the wood pile.' The politicians disfranchised the Negro to get rid of his vote, which was in their way, and they kept the Negro scarecrow bolstered up for fear that the whites might divide and that the Negro might then come back into possession of the ballot.

"The politicians proposed no measures of relief for the great mass of ignorance and poverty in their midst. The modicum of school appropriations was wrung from them, in some instances, by the threats of the better element of the people. They were obstructionists rather than constructionists. One Benjamin Tillman boasted on the floor of the United States Senate that in his state he kept the Negroes 'in their place' by the use of the shot-gun, in defiance of law and the constitution, and that he expected to keep it up. If left alone, the feeling against Negroes would have subsided to some extent and mutual helpfulness prevailed, but the politicians had to have an issue, even at the sacrifice of peace between the races and at the expense of a loss of labor in many sections where it was once plentiful—as many Negroes left for more liberal states, where they not only received better wages but also better treatment. The Southern farmer and business man was paying a dear price for office holders when he stood by the politicians and allowed them to run off Negro labor, by disfranchisement and political oppression. It was paying too much for a whistle of that quality.

"Many Negroes thought, with Bishop Turner and John Temple Graves, that emigration was the solution of the problem; not necessarily emigration from the United States, but emigration individually to states where public sentiment had not been wrought up against them. But the Negro, owing to his ignorance, and also to his affection for the land of his birth, and on account of a peculiar provincialism that narrowed his scope of vision of the world and its opportunities, could not bring himself to leave the South, so far as the great mass was concerned. Then, too, he had been told that the Yankees would not treat him like the Southerner, and Southern newspapers took especial pains to publish full details of all the lynchings that occurred in the North and make suggestive comments on them, in which they endeavored to show that the whole country was down on the Negro, and that while in the South the whites lynched only the one Negro against whom they had become enraged, in the North they mobbed and sought to drive out *all* the Negroes in the community where the crime had been committed. (The two clippings below occurred in the same issue of a Southern paper and showed how, while the North was mobbing a Negro, the South was honoring one.)[4]

---

4.   Negro Torn From Jail By An Ohio Mob.

Shot Dead On The Ground, Then Hanged From Telegraph Pole—
Yells Of Laughter—For Half An Hour The Swinging Corpse Serves
As A Target For The Mob Which Pours Lead Into It, Shrieking With
Delight.

(By the Associated Press.)

Springfield, Ohio, March 7, 1904.—Richard Dixon, a Negro, was shot to death here tonight by a mob for the killing of Policeman Charles Collis, who died today from wounds received at the hands of Dixon on Sunday.

Collis had gone to Dixon's room on the Negro's request. Dixon said his mistress had his clothes in her possession. Collis accompanied Dixon to the room, and in a short time the man and woman engaged in a quarrel, which resulted in Dixon shooting the woman, who is variously known as Anna or Mamie Corbin, in the left breast just over the heart. She fell unconscious at the first shot and Collis jumped towards the Negro to prevent his escape from the room. Dixon then fired four balls into Collis, the last of which penetrated his abdomen. Dixon went immediately to police headquarters and gave himself up. He was taken to jail.

"Instances of white mechanics North who were refusing to work with Negroes, and instances of Northern hotels refusing them shelter were also made the most of and served the purpose of deterring Negro emigration from the Southern States. Frequently some Negro was

---

As soon as Collis' death became known talk of lynching the Negro was heard and tonight a crowd began to gather about the jail.

The mob forced an entrance to the jail by breaking in the east doors with a railroad iron.

At 10:30 the mob melted rapidly and it was the general opinion that no more attempts would be made to force an entrance. Small groups of men, however, could be seen in the shadows of the court house, two adjacent livery stables and several dwelling houses. At 10:45 o'clock the police were satisfied that there was nothing more to fear and they with other officials and newspaper men passed freely in and out of the jail.

Shortly before 11 o'clock a diversion was made by a small crowd moving from the east doors around to the south entrance. The police followed and a bluff was made at jostling them off the steps leading up to the south entrance.

The crowd at this point kept growing, while yells of "hold the police," "smash the doors," "lynch the nigger" were made, interspersed with revolver shots.

All this time the party with the heavy railroad iron was beating at the east door, which shortly yielded to the battering ram, as did the inner lattice iron doors. The mob then surged through the east door, overpowered the sheriff, turnkey and handful of deputies and began the assault on the iron turnstile leading to the cells. The police from the south door were called inside to keep the mob from the cells and in five minutes the south door had shared the fate of the east one.

In an incredibly short time the jail was filled with a mob of 250 men with all the entrances and yard gates blocked by fully 2,500 men, thus making it impossible for the militia to have prevented access to the Negro, had it been on the scene.

The heavy iron partition leading to the cells resisted the mob effectually until cold chisels and sledge hammers arrived, which were only two or three minutes late in arriving. The padlock to the turnstile was broken and the mob soon filled the corridors leading to the cells.

Seeing that further resistance was useless and to avoid the killing of innocent prisoners the authorities consented to the demand of the mob for the right man. He was dragged from his cell to the jail door and thence down the stone steps to a court in the jail yard.

Fearing an attempt on the part of the police to rescue him, the leaders formed a hollow square. Some one knocked the Negro to the ground and those near to him fell back four or five feet. Nine shots were fired into his prostrate body, and satisfied that he was dead, a dozen men grabbed the lifeless body, and with a triumphant cheer the mob surged into Columbia street and marched to Fountain Avenue, one of the principal streets of the town. From here they marched south to the intersection of Main street, and a rope was tied around Dixon's neck. Two men climbed the pole and threw the rope over the topmost crosstie and drew the body about eighteen feet above the street. They then descended and their work was greeted with a cheer.

The fusillade then began and for thirty minutes the body was kept swaying back and forth, from the force of the rain of bullets which was poured into it. Frequently the arms would fly up convulsively when a muscle was struck, and the mob went fairly wild with delight. Throughout it all perfect order was maintained and everyone seemed in the best of humor, joking with his nearest neighbor while re-loading his revolver.

EDWARD A. JOHNSON

brought home dead, or one who had contracted disease in the North came home and died. These occurrences were also used as object lessons and had their effect.

"In fact, the Southern white people did not want the Negroes to leave. They wanted them as domestics, on the farm, and as mechanics. They knew their value as such. 'Be as intelligent, as capable as you may but acknowledge my superiority,' was the unspoken command.

"Many individual Negroes acted on this suggestion and by shrewd foresight managed to accumulate considerable property, and so long as they 'minded their own business,' and 'stayed out of politics' they did well, and had strong personal friends among the white people. Their property rights were recognized to a very large extent, in fact the right of Negroes to hold property was very generally conceded. This was true even to the extent, in several instances, of causing reimbursement for those who were run away from their homes by mobs. In some states laws were passed giving damages to the widows of those who were lynched by mobs, said damages to be paid by the county in which the lynching occurred. In fact the South had long since discovered the Negro's usefulness and the feeling against him partook more of political persecution than race hatred. The paradoxical scheme of retaining six million Negroes in the population with all the rights and duties of citizenship, less social and political standing, was the onus of the problem in the South. Such a scheme as this was bound to breed more or less persecution and lawlessness, as did the slave system. It was a makeshift at best, and though in the main, honestly undertaken, it was impossible of performance.

"The Southern people seemed to have no objection to personal contact with Negroes in a servile capacity. Many Negro women made

---

A Negro Honored.

Columbus, Georgia, Erects A Monument To A Heroic Laborer.

(*By the Associated Press.*)

Macon, Ga., March 9, 1902.—A Columbus, Ga., dispatch to the Telegraph says a marble monument has been erected by the city to the memory of Bragg Smith, the Negro laborer who lost his life last September in a heroic but fruitless effort to rescue City Engineer Robert L. Johnson from a street excavation. On one side is an inscription setting forth the fact, while on the other side is chiseled,

> "*Honor and shame from no condition rise;*
> *Act well thy part, there all the honor lies.*"

their living as 'wet nurses,' and the Southern 'black mammy' had become stereotyped. Then, too, the large number of mulatto children everywhere was some evidence of personal contact, on the part of the men. Negro servants swarmed around the well-to-do Southern home, cooked the food and often slept with the children; the Southerner shook hands with his servants on his return home from a visit and was glad to see them; but if any of these servants managed by industry and tact to rise to higher walks of life, it became necessary, according to the unwritten law, to break off close relations. Yet, in the great majority of cases, the interest and good feeling remained, if the Negro did not become too active politically—in which case he could expect 'no quarter.'

"The subject of lynching became very serious. This evil custom, for a while, seemed to threaten the whole nation. While Negroes were the most common victims, yet the fever spread like a contagion to the lynching of white criminals as well.

"At first it was confined to criminals who committed assaults on women, and to brutal murderers, but it soon became customary to lynch for the slightest offense, so that no man's life was safe if he was unfortunate enough to have had a difficulty with some individual, who had friends enough to raise a mob at night who would go with him to the house of his victim, call him out, and either shoot, or unmercifully beat him. The refusal of the officers of the law to crush out this spirit in its embryonic stage resulted in its growing to such enormous proportions that they found, too late, that they could neither manage nor control it. The officers themselves were afraid of the lynchers.

"The method of lynching Negroes was usually by hanging or by burning at the stake, sometimes in the presence of thousands of people, who came in on excursion trains to see the sight, and, possibly, carry off a trophy consisting of a finger joint, a tooth or a portion of the victim's heart. If the lynching was for a crime committed against a woman, and she could be secured, she was consigned to the task of starting the flames with her own hands. This was supposed to add to the novelty of the occasion.[5]

---

5. BURNING OF NEGROES.

Birmingham, Ala., Special.—The Age-Herald recently published the following letter from Booker T. Washington:

"Within the last fortnight three members of my race have been burned at the stake; of these one was a woman. Not one of the three was charged with any

EDWARD A. JOHNSON

"'Why did not the Negro offer some resistance to these outrages?' you may ask.

"That question, no doubt, is often propounded by those who read of the horrors of this particular period. Different theories are advanced. One is that the Negro was overawed by numbers and resources—that he saw the uselessness of any such attempt. Another theory is that during the whole history of Negro slavery in this country there occurred only one or two rebellions worthy of the name. One was the 'Nat Turner Insurrection' in Southampton County, Virginia, in 1831. This was soon put down and the ringleader hung, together with several of his misguided followers. So it must be concluded, since the Negro

---

crime even remotely connected with the abuse of a white woman. In every case murder was the sole accusation. All of these burnings took place in broad daylight, and two of them occurred on Sunday afternoon in sight of a Christian church.

"In the midst of the nation's prosperous life, few, I fear, take time to consider whither these brutal and inhuman practices are leading us. The custom of burning human beings has become so common as scarcely to attract interest or unusual attention. I have always been among those who condemned in the strongest terms crimes of whatever character committed by members of my race, and I condemn them now with equal severity, but I maintain that the only protection to our civilization is a fair and calm trial of all people charged with crime, and in their legal punishment, if proved guilty. There is no excuse to depart from legal methods. The laws are, as a rule, made by the white people, and their execution is by the hands of the white people so that there is little probability of any guilty colored man escaping. These burnings without trial are in the deepest sense unjust to my race, but it is not this injustice alone which stirs my heart. These barbarous scenes, followed as they are by the publication of the shocking details, are more disgraceful and degrading to the people who influence the punishment than to those who receive it.

"If the law is disregarded when a negro is concerned, will it not soon also be disregarded in the case of the white man? And besides the rule of the mob destroys the friendly relations which should exist between the races and injures and interferes with the material prosperity of the communities concerned.

"Worst of all, these outrages take place in communities where there are Christian churches; in the midst of people who have their Sunday schools, their Christian Endeavor Societies and Young Men's Christian Associations; collections are taken up to send missionaries to Africa and China and the rest of the so-called heathen world.

"Is it not possible for pulpit and press to speak out against these burnings in a manner that will arouse a sentiment that shall compel the mob to cease insulting our courts, our governors and our legal authority, to cease bringing shame and ridicule upon our Christian civilization.

BOOKER T. WASHINGTON.
Tuskegee, Ala

bore two hundred and fifty years of slavery so patiently, and made only a few feeble attempts to liberate himself, that he is not naturally of a rebellious nature—that he easily fits into any place you put him, and with the fatalistic tendency of all barbaric races, except the Indian, makes the best of circumstances. It is possibly true that the Negro would be a slave among us today if some one else had not freed him. The sentiment, 'He who would be free must first himself strike the blow,' did not appeal to him.

"Another reason cited for the Negro's submission so long to oppression both before and since the American Civil War of 1860 to 1865 was his inability to organize. The white man learned this art by thousands of years of experience and of necessary resistance for the protection of those rights which he holds most dear. The Negroes were never able to make any concerted movement in their own behalf. They clashed too easily with one another and any individual would swamp the ship, as it were, to further his own scheme. The 'rule or ruin' policy prevailed and the necessity of the subordination of individuality for the good of the whole was lost in a storm of personal aggrandizement whenever an attempt was made at anything bordering on Negro national organization. This was one of the fruits of slavery, which encouraged jealousy and bickering. Several religious organizations had a successful existence for some time and quite a number of business and benevolent enterprises, but in politics all was chaos. The Negroes cast their ballots one way all of the time; it was known just as well ten years before an election how they would vote, as it was after the ballots were counted. No people of political calibre like that could measure arms with the white man politically; his rebelling in such a condition would have been preposterous. The Negro took his cue in matters of race policy from his white friends—he did not fight until the signal was given by them. No Negro gained any national reputation without first having been recognized by the white race, instead of his own. The Negroes recognized their leaders after the whites picked them out—not before.

"The Negro nature at this time was still a pliable one, after many years of drill training, but it was much more plastic in the days of slavery, and for the first forty years after reconstruction. The master labored to subordinate the will of the slave to his own, to make him like clay in the hands of the potter. In this he had an eye to business. The nearer the slave approached the horse, in following his master's guidance, the nearer perfect he was, and this lesson of putting himself absolutely at the mercy of his master was thoroughly learned, and it was learned easily because there seemed to exist a natural instinctive awe on the part of the Negro for the white man. He had that peculiar fondness for him that the mule has for the horse. You can mount one horse and lead a thousand mules, without bit or bridle, to the ends of the earth.

"The Negro sought to please his master in all things. He had a smile for his frowns and a grin for his kicks. No task was too menial, if done for a white master—he would dance if he was called upon and make sport of the other Negroes, and even pray, if need be, so he could laugh at him. He was trustworthy to the letter, and while occasionally he might help himself to his master's property on the theory of a common ownership, yet woe be unto the other Negro that he caught tampering with his master's goods! He was a 'tattler' to perfection, a born dissembler—a diplomat and a philosopher combined. He was past grand master in the art of carrying his point when he wanted a 'quarter' or fifty cents. He knew the route to his master's heart and pocketbook and traveled it often. He simply made himself so obliging that he could not be refused! It was this characteristic that won him favor in the country from college president down to the lowest scullion. Had he been resentful and vindictive, like the Indian, he would have been deported or exterminated long since.

"The Negro's usefulness had also bound him to the South. The affection that the master and mistress had for the slave was transmitted in the blood of their children.

> *"As unto the bow the cord is,*
> *So unto the man is woman,*
> *Though she bends him, she obeys him,*
> *Though she draws him, yet she follows;*
> *Useless each without the other,"*

applied to the relations between the Negro and his white master. In the Civil War between the states, many a slave followed his master to the front. Here he was often the only messenger to return home. He bore the treasured watch, or ring, or sword, of the fallen soldier, and broke the sad news to the family; and there were black tears as well as white ones spilled on such occasions.

"The white males went to the war leaving the family and farm in charge of the blacks thereon. They managed everything, plowed, sowed, reaped, and sold, and turned over all returns to the mistress. They shared her sorrows and were her protection. When Union soldiers came near, the trusted blacks were diligent in hiding property from the thieves and bummers of the army. They carried the horses to the woods and hid them in the densest swamps, they buried the jewelry and silver and gold plate; they secreted their young mistresses and the members of the family where they could not be found, and not one instance was there ever heard of improper conduct, out of a population of nearly four million slaves; in spite of the fact that the war was being maintained by their masters for the perpetuation of the shackles of slavery on themselves! The Negro was too fond of his master's family to mistreat them, he felt almost a kinship to them. The brutes of later days came from that class of Negroes who had been isolated from the whites, on the quarters of large plantations.

"Was there ever a more glorious record? Did ever a race deserve more fully the affection of another race than these southern Negroes, and did not we owe it to their descendants to save them from both deportation and serfdom?

"You ask, 'Why was it that after the war there was so much race prejudice, in the face of all these facts?'

"The answer to that question is fraught with much weight and bears strongly on the final solution of the Negro problem. The friends of the Negro had this question to battle with from the beginning, for the enemies of the race used every weapon at hand in the long and terrible fight against Negro citizenship.

"To begin with, I will state that after the war the Negro became a free citizen and a voter—he was under no restraint. His new condition gave him privileges that he had never had before; it was not unnatural that he should desire to exercise them. His attempts to do so were resisted by the native whites, but his vote was needed by the white men who had recently come into the South to make it their home—and to get office—and also for his own protection. It was necessary that he should vote to save himself from many of the harsh laws that were being proposed at the time. Some of them were that a Negro should not own land, that a Negro's testimony was incompetent in the courts, that a Negro should not keep firearms for his defense, that he should not engage in business without paying a high and almost prohibitive tax, that he must hire himself out on a farm in January or be sold to the highest bidder for a year, the former owner to have the preference in bidding.

"These laws were unwisely urged by those whites who did not desire to accept the consequences of the war. To make the laws effective, it was thought necessary by their advocates to suppress the Negro voters; for, if they were allowed to vote, there were so many of them, and so many of the whites had been disfranchised because of participation in the war, that defeat was certain. Here is where the bitterness, which for a long time seemed to curse our country, had its origin. The Negroes and their friends were lined up on one side and their opponents on the other.

"The 'Ku Klux Klan' was a secret organization whose purpose was to frighten and intimidate Negroes and thus prevent their voting. It had branch organizations in the different Southern states during the reconstruction period. When the members went out on raids, they wore disguises; some had false heads with horns and long beards, some represented his satanic majesty, some wore long gowns, others wrapped themselves in sheets of different colors, and all sorts of hideous shapes and forms, with masks representing the heads of different animals, such as goats, cows and mules. They proceeded on the principle of using mild means first, but when that failed, they did not hesitate to resort to harsher methods. The object seemed to be only to so frighten Negroes that they would not attempt to vote. But in carrying out this scheme they often met resistance, whereupon many outrages were perpetrated upon people who made a stand for their rights under the law of the land. In obstinate cases and toward the end of their careers "klans" would visit Negro cabins at night and terrify the inmates by whipping them, hanging them up by their thumbs, and sometimes killing them. Many Negroes who assumed to lead among their people were run from one county into another. Some were run out of their states, and even white men who led the Negroes in thickly settled Negro counties were driven out.

"The story was told of one case where a white man named Stephens, the recognized political leader of the Negroes as well as a few whites, in one of the states, was invited into one of the lower rooms of the courthouse of his county while a political meeting by his opponents was in progress above, and there told he must agree to leave the county and quit politics or be killed then and there. He refused to do either, whereupon two physicians, with others who were present, tied him, laid him on a table and opened his jugular veins and bled him to death in buckets provided for the occasion. Meanwhile the stamping of feet and the yelling above, where the speaking was going on, was tremendous, being prearranged to deaden any outcry that he might make. It is said that Stephens's last words before he was put on the table were a request that he might go to the window and take a final look at his home, which was only a few rods away. This was granted, and as he looked his wife passed out of the house and his children were playing in the yard. Stephens's dead body was found by a Negro man who suspected something wrong and climbed to the window of the room in search for him.

"Such acts as these spread terror among the Negro population, as well as bad feeling, and dug a wide political pit between the Negro and the Democratic party which organized these methods of intimidation.[6] The 'Ku Klux Klan' was finally annihilated by the strong hand of President Grant, who filled the South with sufficient militia to suppress it. A favorite means of evading the arrests made by the militia was to have the prisoners released on *habeas corpus* by the native judges. To stop this the writ of *habeas corpus* was suspended by some of the provisional governors. One governor who did this was impeached by the Democratic party when it returned to power and he died broken hearted, without the removal of his disabilities. You can easily see from these facts how the political differences between the Negro and the Democratic party arose."

Here my paper ended. When I had read it over to Dr. Newell, he rose and went over to his desk, saying,

"While looking over some old papers belonging to my grandfather, I found the following article inside of an old book. On it is a statement that it was written in the year 1902 and republished in 1950. I have often desired to get at the true status of this question, and when I found this my interest was doubly aroused. The so-called Negro problem was truly a most crucial test of the foundation principles of our government a century ago, and I feel proud of my citizenship in so great a country when I reflect that we have come through it all with honor and that finally truth has won out and we are able at last to treat the Negro with justice and humanity, according to the principles of Christianity! This problem tested our faith as with fire."

He handed me the article, and gave his attention to other matters until I had read it:—

---

6. Tourgée relates this incident in "A Fool's Errand."

EDWARD A. JOHNSON

"Reconstruction and Negro Government.

"In the ten years culminating with the decade ending in 1902, the American Negroes have witnessed well nigh their every civil right invaded. They commenced the struggle as freemen in 1865; at the close of the civil war both races in the South began life anew, under changed conditions— neither one the slave of the other, except in so far as he who toils, as Carlyle says, is slave to him who thinks. Under the slave system the white man had been the thinker and the Negro the toiler. The idea that governed both master and slave was that the slave should have no will but that of his master.

"The fruits of this system began to ripen in the first years of freedom, when the Negro was *forced* to think for himself. For two hundred and forty years his education and training had been directed towards the suppression of his will. He was fast becoming an automaton. He was taught religion to some extent, but a thoughtless religion is little better than mockery and this it must have been when even to read the Bible in some states was a crime. It is, therefore, not surprising that freedom's new suit fitted the recently emancipated slave uncomfortably close; he hardly knew which way to turn for fear he would rend a seam. Consultation with his former owners was his natural recourse in adjusting himself to new conditions.

"In North Carolina a meeting was called at the capital of the state by the leading colored men, and their former masters, and the leading white men were invited to come forward, to take the lead and to tell them what was best for them to do. It is a lamentable fact that the thinking white men did not embrace this opportunity to save their state hundreds of lives that were afterwards sacrificed during reconstruction. Many other evils of the period, might have been thus averted. It was a fatal blunder that cost much in money and blood, and, so far as North Carolina is concerned, if the Negroes in reconstruction were misled it was the fault of those who were invited and refused this opportunity to take hold and direct them properly.

"The Negro, turned from the Southern white man's refusal, followed such leaders as he could find. In some instances these proved to be corrupt camp followers, in others ambitious and unscrupulous Southern men who made the Negroes stepping stones to power or pelf. The Negroes of the state received very little of the honor or harvest of reconstruction, but very much of dishonor, and they are now charged with the sins both of omission and commission of that period. A pliant tool he may have been in the hands of demagogues, yet in the beginning he sought the leadership of wise men. In this he showed a noble purpose which at least relieves him—whatever was charged to his account afterwards—of the charge of malicious intent.

"Here is a list of prominent white leaders in North Carolina who controlled the ship of state for the first ten years after the war, from 1869 to 1876:

"Wm. E. Rodman (Southern white), Judge Dick (Southern white), W. W. Holden, Governor (Southern white), Byron Baffin (Southern white), Henry Martindale (Ohio white), Gen'l Ames (Northern), G. Z. French, legislator (Maine), Dr. Eugene Grissom, Superintendent Insane Asylum Raleigh, North Carolina (Southern white), Tyre York, legislator and party leader (Southern white), Governor Graham (Southern white), Judge Brooks (Southern white), S. J. Carrow (Southern white).

"This list shows that those who had the reins of government in hand were not Negroes. The truth is, that if the team went wrong the fault was that of the white drivers and not that of the Negro passengers who, to say the most, had only a back seat in the wagon of state.

"But the enemies of Negro suffrage and advocates of the mistakes of reconstruction avow that the sway of reconstruction demagoguery could never have prevailed but for Negro suffrage; that had the Negro not been a voter he could never have been made the tool of demagogues. This is obvious but the argument is sufficiently met by the fact that the Negroes offered the brain and culture of the South the opportunity of taking charge of affairs. Instead of doing so they stiffened their necks against Negro suffrage, the Howard Amendment, and the other propositions of the government at Washington, looking towards the reconstruction of the lately seceded states. If there had been less resistance there would have been less friction, but the South had its own ideas of how the thing should be done and resisted any others to the point of a revolution which had to be put down by government troops. The government's plans were carried finally at the point of the bayonet, when they might have gone through smoothly, had the Negro's call for Southern leadership been heeded. Had this been done, the 'Ku-Klux' would never have developed. The South came back into the Union, 'overpowered,' it said, 'but not conquered.' So far as the Negro question is concerned that is true but in other matters the South is essentially loyal. Although it came back pledged never to deprive any citizen of his rights and privileges 'on account of color or previous condition of servitude,' it is now engaged in a bold and boasting attempt to do this very thing. Louisiana, Mississippi, Alabama, South Carolina, North Carolina and Virginia have all adopted amendments to their constitutions which practically nullify the Fourteenth and Fifteenth Amendments to the United States Constitution, which the honor of these states was pledged not to do when they were re-admitted into the Union at the close of the war of secession! In Virginia the amendment was established without submitting the question to the popular vote. To secure these amendments in other states, fraud and intimidation is alleged to have been used, and the Southern states that have not amended their constitutions have effected the same results by a system of political jugglery with the Negro's ballots.

"The Southern states seem to live in mortal dread of the Negro with a ballot. They imagine a Pandora's box of evils will open upon them if the Negro is allowed to vote. This feeling arises more from the fact that the whites want the offices than from any other cause. Past experience shows that Negroes have never attempted to claim all of the offices, even where they did ninety-nine per cent. of the voting. It is a notable fact that in North Carolina during the reconstruction times, when few white men voted and Negroes had a monopoly of the ballot, that white men were put forward for official positions. The same condition existed in the period from 1894 to 1898, during the 'Fusion Movement,' when out of ninety-six counties, each of which had three commissioners elected by the people, only four counties out of the ninety-six had a Negro commissioner; and the commissioners in two-thirds of the counties were elected principally by Negro votes—in many of the eastern counties, almost wholly by them. Out of ninety-six counties the Negroes never demanded a single sheriff or a mayor of a city, town or village. There were a few Negro magistrates in the eastern counties, but always more white ones near by and under a provision of a North Carolina statute any defendant who thinks he cannot get justice before the magistrate in whose court he is summoned for trial, can have his case moved to some other justice.

"The evils of reconstruction were due to the general demoralization which followed the Civil War, rather than to the Negro. War is 'hell' and so is its aftermath.

"Another pet assertion of the opponents of Negro suffrage is that Negro government is expensive. Those who despair of reaching the American conscience in any other way hope to do so through the pocket argument, commercialism if you please. This argument, like the others, has no facts for a basis. It is a phantom, a delusion and is intended to affect the business element of the North, which people sometimes mistakenly think has more respect for prices than principles. It will not do, however, to listen to the siren of commercialism whose songs are composed by advocates of Negro disfranchisement. There is method in the spell she would bring upon you, and her story is literally nothing but a song.

"The truth is that during the whole period of the 'Fusion Movement' North Carolina never had a more economical government—taxes then were 93c. on a hundred dollar valuation; taxes now are $1.23. North Carolina six per cent. bonds then sold for $1.10; they now sell for $1.09. The Fusion government made the state penitentiary self-supporting; the white supremacy government has run it into debt to the amount of $50,000. Under the Fusion government, most of the counties paid off their debts and had a surplus in their treasuries for the first time since the war. Under the Fusion government more miles of railroad were built than in any period of the same length before or since, more cotton factories were established; one of them being owned and operated by Negroes. A silk mill operated entirely by Negro labor, from foremen down, was also established. The fees of public officers were cut down about one-third. These are some of the phases of the Fusion government—a government based almost entirely on Negro votes— that the enemies of Negro suffrage do not discuss.

"It is useless to refer to the period of reconstruction to disprove the theory that Negro suffrage would entail an expensive government on the South, when we have the recent experiment in North Carolina before us. For the sake of argument, we might admit that the Negro was unfit for suffrage forty years ago, but that by no means proves that he is unfit now. Forty years of experience under American institutions have taught him many lessons. He is no longer the 'child-man,' as the white supremacy advocates call him. These people are as false in their theories as were the pro-slavery advocates who maintained the absurd proposition that if the Negro was emancipated he would soon perish, for want of sufficient ability to feed and clothe himself. Forty years after emancipation—about as long as Moses was in the wilderness—in spite of these false prophecies, we can now find some of the sons of the prophets fearing and foretelling, not that the Negroes will perish, but that they will outstrip them in the race of life! So the white man in the new constitution is to be allowed to vote on his 'grand-daddy's'[7] merits and the Negro must vote on his own.

"These politicians were afraid to base the right to vote on merit, as they feared the Negro would win.[8] Among these people a Negro has to be twice as smart as a white man to merit the same favors, yet in a recent

---

7. The grandfather clause in the North Carolina constitution, as recently amended, gives illiterate whites the right to vote if their grandfathers voted *prior to* 1867. The negroes were enfranchised in 1867 and their grandfathers therefore could not have voted prior to that time. So, while all negroes must be able to read and write the constitution, in order to vote, the illiterate white man may do so because his "grand-daddy" voted prior to 1867.

8. As Mr. A. V. Dockery, who is a competent authority, so tersely said in the New York Age, June 23, 1904, the Negro has been practically the only natural Republican in the South. That a considerable number of soldiers were furnished by the South to the Union army during the Civil War is not contested, and proves little as to political conditions then and for several decades later. It is well known that the mountain section of North Carolina, Tennessee, Kentucky and Virginia sent many soldiers to the Northern army; it may not be so well known that Madison county, North Carolina, the home of Judge Pritchard, contributed more soldiers to the Union cause, in proportion to population, than any other county in the whole United States.

It was not asserted that all those soldiers were then, or afterwards became, Republicans. Before the emancipation, there were some Republicans in this sparsely settled section, it is true, but aggressive Republicanism in the South *got its impetus and had its birth* in the actual emancipation, not necessarily the enfranchisement, of the Negro.

Yet when this remnant of white Republicans could no longer protect the Negro in his right to vote, and successive Congresses supinely consented to his disfranchisement, the South's contribution to Congress consisted of less than half a dozen Republican congressmen, and these only from the aforesaid mountain district.

The Negro, being held up as a terrible hobgoblin to political white folks, it was necessary to destroy his citizenship; which was accomplished by wily and cruel means. About one and a half million citizens were disfranchised and yet we have a paradox. This vast mass of manhood is represented in Congress—in what way? By arbitrarily nullifying the constitution of the Nation. It was the boast in 1861 that one Southern man could whip ten Yankees. May not this same class of Southern politicians now proudly and truly boast that one Southern vote is equal to ten Yankee votes?

Have the ten million American Negroes any more direct representation in Congress than the ten million Filipinos?

Civil Service examination in Atlanta 19 Negroes out of 40 passed, while only 26 whites out of 115 succeeded. In an examination of law students by the Supreme Court of North Carolina only 40 per cent. of the whites passed, while 100 per cent. of the colored got licenses. A hundred other illustrations might be made showing the speciousness of the arguments put forth as to Negro incompetency. The fact is that there is no use in arguing such a proposition. The effort made to suppress the Negro has no just basis. There has simply been a determination to *do it*, right or wrong. The advocates of white supremacy who watch the current of events, have seen that the decitizenization of the Negro can be accomplished with the shot-gun, without trouble to themselves, and they have accomplished the task. They have asked to be let alone with the Negro problem; they *have* been let alone since 1876, when the Republican party dropped the Negro question as an issue. Since that time they have been politically tying the Negroes' hands. Realizing his industrial usefulness, the aim has been to eliminate him from politics and at the same time use him as a tax-payer and a producer. The paradoxical task of defining his citizenship as that of one with all the burdens and duties, less the rights and privileges thereof, has been quite successfully performed.

"The white supremacy advocates seem to have selected a propitious period for this work—a time when the Negro's friends in the Republican party are occupied with similar problems in Cuba and the Philippines.

In 1896 there was only one party in the South and its primaries elected the congressmen. Seven congressional districts in South Carolina cast a total of less than 40,000 votes for the seven congressmen elected to the Fifty-seventh Congress.

For the same Congress, Minnesota cast a total of 276,000 votes for seven congressmen, an average of 39,428 votes each; whereas the average in South Carolina was less than 6,000 votes per congressman. In other words, one South Carolina congressman is equal to seven of the Minnesota article.

If every "lily white" Democrat in the old fighting South during the last decade of the twentieth century (the "lily white" age) had received an office, no benefit for the so-called Negro party would have been attained, and the South would have remained as solid as ever. The men there who amassed fortunes as a result of the Republican policy of protection, remained Democrats, notwithstanding the elimination of the Negro as a political factor. The "lily white" party had no other principle except greed for office. It was a delicious sham and the people knew it, white and blacks alike. It was distinctly proven that as long, and no longer, as there was any Federal office in the South to be filled there was a Democrat or a "lily white" handy and anxious to fill it and willing to keep his mouth shut only during the occupation.

It is not surprising, therefore, that President Roosevelt early in his administration gave the "lily-white" party to understand that it was *persona non grata* at the White House. As a true patriot and an honest man he could not have done less.

EDWARD A. JOHNSON

'If the Republicans deny self-government to the Philippines, Porto Rico and Cuba,' inquire the Southerners, 'why haven't we the right to do the same to Negroes? Why allow Negroes in the South to rule and deny the same to Negroes in Hawaii?' are questions they are asking with some force. Whatever else the advocates of white supremacy may lack they are not lacking in shrewdness. Their disfranchising schemes have flaunted themselves under the very nose of the government, and bid it defiance in the National Senate with unmistakable boldness, since the Spanish-American War and the policy growing out of it. However there seems to be a man in the White House who wants to set no example that white supremacy can follow; so far as his indicated policy in dealing with Cuba was concerned, President Roosevelt determined that the black people of Cuba should be free.

"But the subordination of the Negro cannot last, there will always be white people in this country who will believe in his equality before the law. These principles are too firmly entrenched in the hearts of Americans to be utterly subverted. They are the bed rock on which the government was founded—on which the Civil War was maintained. Too much of blood and treasure has been spent now to go backwards. These principles have been established at too great a cost to abandon them so soon. It is true that the white supremacy advocates seem now in control of the situation, but that also seemed true of the advocates of slavery before the war. While the enemies of liberty have always been cunning, yet like all other advocates of false doctrines who get power, they usually abuse it; the South might have held her slaves for many years longer, had she not overstepped the mark by trying to force the institution on the North. She attempted to extend slavery into new territories, she even attempted to capture her slaves in the streets of anti-slavery cities like Boston, by the Fugitive Slave Law—under the very noses of the abolitionists! Had the pro-slavery people been satisfied with restricted slavery, the abolitionists might have had harder work in dethroning the institution.

"If the question of lynching had been confined to Negroes guilty of assaults on females some justification might exist, but it has been extended to all crimes; and not satisfied with hanging, burning by slow fire has been substituted, accompanied by stabbing, the cutting off of finger joints, the digging out of eyes, and other torture.

"On the question of civil equality, the 'Jim-crow' system has not sufficed; like the horse leech, they continually call for more. If practiced only in the South it might stand, but an attempt has been made to cover the country, and the President himself must not treat a colored gentleman otherwise than as a scullion—according to the advocates of white supremacy. In their doctrine *all* Negroes are to be humiliated. This tendency to dictate to others and go to extremes is characteristic, and it means that we may always depend on this class of individuals to go too far, and by over-stepping the mark to turn the country against them.

"If a fool has rope enough the end is easy to see."

AFTER READING THE ARTICLE, I turned to the Doctor, and said, "These statements are essentially correct, according to my recollection of those times, and I will say further that there were grave doubts one hundred years ago as to the permanency of our institutions under the strain of the Negro problem; and no less prominent was the labor agitation or the war between capital and labor. It is a happy realization for me to return to my country and find these questions peaceably adjusted and that the South, which was for a long time considered obdurate on this subject, has led in bringing about this happy solution, in spite of the prophecies of many writers like this one. But the problem I have been laboring with ever since my second advent, as it were, is, how was it all done?

"Well, we Southern people changed our leaders. We took men of noble character; men who appealed to reason and humanity, rather than pandered to the lowest passions of the people," he said.

"Tell me, Dr. Newell, how the labor question was settled and how the labor unions learned to leave off discriminating against Negroes. According to my best recollections the American labor organizations, almost without exception, excluded Negro members."

"Yes," replied Dr. Newell, "that is correct, as I have gleaned from the history of your times, but—as all injustice must—this particular instance followed the fixed rule and finally gave way to truth. Such discriminations were incompatible with the spirit and trend of our government. The labor leaders, however, yielded in the end more from a sense of necessity than of justice to the Negro. As Lincoln said, the nation could not exist half slave and half free, and as Blaine said, in his famous Augusta speech, no imaginary line could continue to divide free labor from serf labor. The labor leaders found, after serious second thought, that it would be better to emancipate Negro labor than to lend their efforts towards keeping it in serfdom. For a long time the labor organizations desired the Negroes deported, as a solution of the problem for themselves alone. They found various influences, especially capital, opposed to this; as one writer put it, 'the Dollar was no respecter of persons and would as soon hop into the hands of a black man, in consideration of the performance of a service, as in those of a white one.' Capital wanted the work done and the man who could do it the cheapest and best was the man that got the Dollar every time. This phase of the question was a constant menace to organized labor, and finally caused a revolution in its tactics. White labor began to see that it would be better to lift the Negro up to the same scale with itself, by admitting him into their organization, than to seek his debasement. If Negroes were in a condition to work for fifty cents per day and would do so, and capital would employ them, then white men must accept the same terms or get no work! This, followed to its last analysis, meant that white laborers must provide for their families and educate their children on fifty cents per day, if the Negroes could do it."

"Did not the South object to the organization of Negro labor?" I asked.

"The Southern people, at first, strongly objected.

"The laboring white people of the South have made serious blunders in their position on the Negro problem, having acted all along on the presumption that the proper solution was to 'keep the Negro down.' Towards this end, they bent their best energies, under the mistaken idea of conserving their own interests, not realizing the all-important fact that as long as there was a large number of Negroes in their midst who would work for only fifty cents per day as above stated, and capital was disposed to employ them, just so long would every laboring white man have to accept the same wages as the Negro.

"The intelligent solution of the problem was found by making the Negro see what his interests were, by taking him into the labor unions, where he could be educated up to an intelligent appreciation of the value of his labor; instead of seeking further to degrade him by oppression, with the consequent result of lowering the white man's scale of wages. Further it has been found that oppression does not oppress when aimed at the Negro—he rather thrives under it. In those communities where he was most oppressed and the hand of every laboring white man seemed to be against him, the Negro thrived and prospered to a marked degree. Oppression simply drives negroes together, they concentrate their trade in their own stores and spend their wages among themselves to a greater extent than otherwise—and thus it more often than otherwise happened, that Negro laborers as a mass, in such communities, lived in better homes, and educated their children better than the white laborers. The eyes of the Southern white laboring men began to see this point and a change of base took place, and now they are and have been for a long time, seeking to elevate the Negro laborer to their own standard to keep him from pulling them down—a most intelligent view of the matter!

"The South had congratulated itself on being free from the strikes and lock-outs caused by organized labor in the North. Their contention was that the Negroes could not act intelligently in any organization, and that serious consequences would certainly follow. But all such predictions failed to materialize after the Negroes were organized. The work of organizing did not stop with their admission into labor unions but courses of instruction were mapped out and competent people were employed to drill the members in the principles of the order; and, so far as possible, in the advanced methods of handling tools. The result was the creation of a much better class of workmen, better wages and better living for all.

"The unions also opened their doors to women in separate meetings. Schools of Domestic Science were established and those who employed servants soon found that they could leave the household and kitchen work to a master-hand. The wives and mothers of employers were emancipated from constantly 'overseeing.' There was a vast difference between the professional domestic servant, who needed only orders, which would be carried out faithfully, and the 'blunderbuss,' who was continually at sea in the absence of the directing hand and mind of her mistress. The Southern people began to recognize the difference, and soon became the firm champions of the new system, and welcomed the new efforts of the labor unions as a blessing rather than a curse."

"But, Doctor, am I to understand that there are no labor problems at all in the country at present?"

"No, not exactly that; organized labor still has its problems, but you must remember that they are not of the same character as those of a hundred years ago. The essentials of life, such as coal, iron, oil and other natural products are now handled by the National Government, and the government is pledged to see to it that labor in the production of these commodities is paid a fair share of the surplus accruing from sales. No attempt at profit is allowed; the management is similar to that of the Post Office Department, which has been conducted from the beginning for the convenience of the people, and not for revenue to the Government. The workmen are paid well and the cost to the consumer is lessened by discarding the profits that formerly went into private purses. We have no more strikes and lock-outs; the chief concern of the labor unions now is to raise their less skillful members to a higher standard (for a long time this effort was especially directed toward the Negro members), and to assist those who, because of infirmity and disease, find themselves incapacitated for further service. It may be well said that the problem of 'wherewithal shall we be clothed' is solved in this country, so far as organized labor is concerned, and more time is now left for the perfection of skill and individual improvement."

"A delightful situation, as compared with the past as I recollect it to be," I remarked—"when labor was paid barely enough to live on, while enormous wealth was being accumulated in the hands of a few fortunate people who happened to be born into opportunities—or, better still, born rich.

"As I remember the past, the laboring people in coal and iron mines earned barely enough for subsistence and their hours of toil were so long that anything like self-improvement was impossible. They were in a continual row with their employers, who revelled in luxury and rebelled against a 10 per cent. increase in wages, and who in many instances, rather than pay it, would close down the mines until their workmen were starved into submission. I never could reconcile myself to the logic of the principle that it was lawful for capital to thus oppress labor. I think the legal maxim of *sic utere tuo ut alienum non laedas* (so use your own as not to injure another) applies with force in this instance. The application of it is usually made in suits for damages, where one person has injured another by negligence. But the force of the maxim is applicable to capital as well, and he who would use money (though in fact it be *legally* his own) to oppress others has violated both the letter and spirit of the maxim. In saying this I would not be understood as indulging in that sickly sentimentality which despises all rich people simply because they are rich, but rather to condemn the illegitimate use of riches. A rich man can be a blessing as well as a curse to his community, and I am indeed happy to learn and see for myself that this is now the rule, rather than the exception, as formerly.

"There is another phase of the question that you have not yet referred to. What is the condition of the farm laborers of the Southern States?" I asked. "When I left they were working from sunrise to sunset, the men earning fifty cents and the women thirty-five cents per day, and they lived in huts with mud chimneys—often a family of six or eight in one room. They had a three months' school during the winter season, when there were no crops, and these were not too often taught by skilled teachers. Has their condition improved so that it is in keeping with the times?"

At this juncture the Doctor was called out of the room before he could reply.

While waiting for him to return, I had a surprise. His private secretary came in and seated himself at a phonographic typewriter which took down the words in shorthand, typewrote them on a sheet for preservation in the office, and at the same time sent the letter by telephone to its destination. But my surprise was awakened by the fact that this private secretary was a Negro; not full black, but mixed blood—in color, between an Indian and a Chinaman. I ascertained from this young man that it was now "quite common" for Southern white men of large affairs to employ Negroes for higher positions in their offices, counting rooms, and stores. (They had a precedent for this in the custom of the Romans, who used their educated Greek slaves in this way.) He also told me that the matter of social equality was not mentioned. He naturally associated with his own people. He simply wanted to do his work faithfully, and neither expected nor asked to sit by his employer's fireside. In a word, he showed that to give the Negro an education need not necessarily "turn his head."[9]

The young man said, "Our theory has kept the two races pure and has developed both the Saxon and the Negro types and preserved the best traits of each."

I noticed that the subdued look of the old time Negro was absent and that, without any attempt at display, this man possessed

---

9. A. A. Gunby, Esq., a member of the Louisiana bar, in a recently published address on Negro education, read before the Southern Educational Association, which met in Atlanta, 1892, took diametrically opposite ground to those who oppose higher education because it will lead to the amalgamation of the races. Mr. Gunby said: "The idea that white supremacy will be endangered by Negro education does not deserve an answer. The claim that their enlightenment will lead to social equality and amalgamation is equally untenable. The more intelligent the Negro becomes the better he understands the true relations and divergences of the races, the less he is inclined to social intermingling with the whites. Education will really emphasize and widen the social gulf between the whites and blacks to the great advantage of the State, for it is a heterogeneous, and not a homogeneous, people that make a republic strong and progressive."

EDWARD A. JOHNSON

"le grande air" which is a coveted attribute in the highest walks of life. I had already observed that an advance in civilization produced more individuality and more personal freedom in choosing one's associates. It was not expected that a man was the social equal of another because he worked at the same bench with him, or rode in the same car on the railroad. That was now considered the postulate of an ignoramus.

Individuality is a marked development of advanced civilization—of this I have always been aware, the more so since witnessing the changes wrought during my absence. Individuality gives room for thought, out of which is born invention and progress. When the individual is not allowed to separate from the crowd in thought and action, the aggregate will, the aggregate thought, is his master and he "dare not venture for fear of a fall." Progress is measured only by the degree of swiftness made by the mass. Some individuals may be able to make better speed, but the mass holds them back. Four horses are pulling a load; two may be able to go faster than the others, but the speed of the team is measured by the speed of the slowest horse.

This does not always appear apropos of the progress of communities, for a community may be led by a few progressive spirits who seem to reflect upon it their own standard and tone, but the less progressive members of such a community have merely subordinated their wills for the time being and may on any occasion see fit to exercise them; and at this point the illustration becomes true again.

"Now," said Doctor Newell, on his return, "I am sorry our conversation was interrupted, but let us proceed. I believe you desired to ask me some questions about the Negro farm laborers, did you not?"

I replied that I did, and recalled my statement as to their condition when I last knew of them.

"Oh, it is very different from that now, Mr. Twitchell. Many changes; many, many, have occurred! You will recall that, about the time you left, the different Southern states were re-reconstructing themselves, as it were, by making amendments to their constitutions which virtually disfranchised a large proportion of the Negro voters—enough to put the offices of the states absolutely into the hands of white men, as outlined in the magazine article you have just read, and as you stated in your brochure for the Bureau of Public Utility. Some passages from a book I have on the subject may remind you of the discussion of this question that was going on then."

Signifying to his secretary what he wanted, he read to me the following excerpts from the history of those times:

"Negro Disfranchisement

"What Dr. F. A. Noble Thinks

"In civil as in business affairs there is nothing so foolish as injustice and oppression; there is nothing so wise as righteousness. By the letter of the amended Constitution, by the spirit and aim of the amendments, and by all the principles of our American democracy, the Negro is in possession of the elective franchise. Men differ in their views as to whether it was good policy to confer this right upon him at the time and in the way, and especially to the extent to which it was done; but the right was conferred, and it is now his. To deprive him of this right, for no other reason than that he is a Negro, is to nullify the fundamental law of the land, discredit one of the most sacred results of Emancipation, and flaunt contempt in the face of the idea of a government of the people and by the people and for the people. To discourage the Negro from attempting to exercise the right of the ballot is to belittle him in his own estimation, put him at a serious disadvantage in the estimation of others, and by so much remand him back to the old condition of servitude from which he was rescued at such cost to the nation. Wrong done to the colored race involves the white race in the catastrophe which must follow. To withhold justice is worse than to suffer injustice. A people deprived of their rights by the state will not long be faithful to their duties to the state.

"What Hon. Carl Schurz Thinks

"That the suppression of the Negro franchise by direct or indirect means is in contravention of the spirit and intent of the Fifteenth Amendment to the Constitution of the United States hardly admits of doubt. The evident intent of the Constitution is that the colored people shall have the right of suffrage on an equal footing with the white people. The intent of the provisions of the State Constitutions in question, as avowed by many Southern men, is that the colored people shall not vote. However plausible it may be demonstrated by ingenious argument that the provisions in the State Constitutions are not in conflict with the National Constitution, or that if they were their purpose could not be effectively thwarted by judicial decisions, yet it remains true that by many, if not by all, of their authors they were expressly designed to defeat the universally known and recognized intent of a provision of the national Constitution. * * *

"The only plausible reason given for that curtailment of their rights is that it is not in the interest of the Southern whites to permit the blacks to vote. I will not discuss here the moral aspect of the question whether A may deprive B of his rights if A thinks it in his own interest to do so, and the further question, whether the general admission of such a principle would not banish justice from the earth and eventually carry human society back into barbarism. I will rather discuss the question whether under existing circumstances it would really be the true interest of the Southern whites generally to disfranchise the colored people. * * *

"Negro suffrage is plausibly objected to on the ground that the great bulk of the colored population of the South are very ignorant. This is true. But the same is true of a large portion of the white population. If the suffrage is dangerous in the hands of certain voters on account of their ignorance, it is as dangerous in the hands of ignorant whites as in the hands of ignorant blacks. To remedy this two things might be done: To establish an educational test for admission to the suffrage, excluding illiterates; and, secondly, to provide for systems of public instruction so as to gradually do away with illiteracy—subjecting whites and blacks alike to the same restrictions and opening to them the same opportunities. * * *

"But most significant and of evil augury is the fact that with many of the Southern whites a well-educated colored voter is as objectionable as an ignorant one, or even more objectionable, simply on account of his color. It is, therefore, not mere dread of ignorance in the voting body that arouses the Southern whites against the colored voters. It is race antagonism, and that race antagonism presents a problem more complicated and perplexing than most others, because it is apt to be unreasoning. It creates violent impulses which refuse to be argued with.

"The race antipathy now heating the Southern mind threatens again to curtail the freedom of inquiry and discussion there—perhaps not to the same extent, but sufficiently to produce infinite mischief by preventing an open-minded consideration of one of the most important interests. * * * And here is the crucial point: *There will be a movement either in the direction of reducing the Negroes to a permanent condition of* *serfdom—the condition of the mere plantation hand, 'alongside of the mule,' practically without any rights of citizenship—or a movement in the direction of recognizing him as a citizen in the true sense of the term. One or the other will prevail.*

"That there are in the South strenuous advocates of the establishment of some sort of semi-slavery cannot be denied. Governor Vardaman, of Mississippi, is their representative and most logical statesman. His extreme utterances are greeted by many as the bugle-blasts of a great leader. We constantly read articles in Southern newspapers and reports of public speeches made by Southern men which bear a striking resemblance to the pro-slavery arguments I remember to have heard before the Civil War, and they are brought forth with the same passionate heat and dogmatic assurance to which we were then accustomed—the same assertion of the Negro's predestination for serfdom; the same certainty that he will not work without 'physical compulsion'; the same contemptuous rejection of Negro education as a thing that will only unfit him for work; the same prediction that the elevation of the Negro will be the degradation of the whites; the same angry demand that any advocacy of the Negro's rights should be put down in the South as an attack upon the safety of Southern society and as treason to the Southern cause. * * *

"Thus may it be said, without exaggeration, that by striving to keep up in the Southern States a condition of things which cannot fail to bring forth constant irritation and unrest; which threatens to burden the South with another 'peculiar institution,' by making the bulk of its laboring force again a clog to progressive development, and to put the South once more in a position provokingly offensive to the moral sense and the enlightened spirit of the world outside, the reactionists are the worst enemies the Southern people have to fear. * * *

"A body of high-minded and enlightened Southerners may gradually succeed in convincing even many of the most prejudiced of their people that white ignorance and lawlessness are just as bad and dangerous as black ignorance and lawlessness; that black patriotism, integrity, ability, industry, usefulness, good citizenship and public spirit are just as good and as much entitled to respect and reward as capabilities and virtues of the same name among whites; that the rights of the white man under the Constitution are no more sacred than those of the black man; that neither white nor black can override the rights of the other without eventually endangering his own; and that the Negro question can finally be settled so as to stay settled only on the basis of the fundamental law of the land as it stands, by fair observance of that law and not by any tricky circumvention of it. Such a campaign for truth and justice, carried on by the high-minded and enlightened Southerners without any party spirit—rather favoring the view that whites as well as blacks should divide their votes according to their inclinations between different political parties—will promise the desired result in the same measure as it is carried on with gentle, patient and persuasive dignity, but also with that unflinching courage which is, above all things, needed to assert that most important freedom—the freedom of inquiry and discussion against traditional and deep-rooted prejudice—a courage which can be daunted neither by the hootings of the mob nor by the supercilious jeers of fashionable society, but goes steadily on doing its work with indomitable tenacity of purpose.

"What The 'New York Evening Post' Thinks

"THIS ANALYSIS OF EXISTING CONDITIONS and tendencies in the South is one to which the South itself and the entire nation should give heed. Mr. Schurz clearly perceives a dangerous drift. Slavery ideas are again asserting themselves. The movement to extinguish the Negro's political rights is unconcealed. By craftily devised and inequitable laws the suffrage is taken from him. With all this go naturally the desire and purpose to keep him forever 'alongside the mule.' Negro education is looked upon with increasing hostility. Every door of hope opening into the professions is slammed in the face of black men merely because they are black. The South works itself up into hysterics over the President's spontaneous recognition of manhood under a black skin. While philanthropists and teachers are laboring to raise the Negro to the full level of citizenship, an open and determined effort is making at the South to thrust him back into serfdom. As Mr. Schurz says, the issue is upon the country, for one tendency or the other must prevail.

"It is his view of the great urgency of the juncture which leads him to address a moving appeal to the South's best. He implores its leading men to bestir themselves to prevent the lamentable injustice which is threatened, and partly executed. By withstanding the mob; by upholding the law; by ridding themselves of the silly dread of 'social equality'; by contending for Negro education of the broadest sort; by hailing every step upward which the black man may take; by insisting upon the equality of all men before the law, they can, Mr. Schurz argues forcibly, do much to save the South and the country from the disgrace and calamity of a new slavery. To this plea every humane patriot will add his voice. Mr. Schurz's paper is also a challenge to the mind and conscience of the North. Unless they, too, respond to the cause of the Negro—which today is the cause of simple justice—it will languish and die.

"What 'The Outlook' Thinks

"It must not be forgotten that the so-called race question is the only capital which a small group of Southern politicians of the old school still possess. They have no other questions or issues; they depend upon the race question for a livelihood, and they use every occasion to say the most extreme things and to set the match to all the inflammable material in the South. To these politicians several occurrences which have happened lately have been a great boon, and they are making the most of them. But there is a large, influential and growing group of Southern men, loyal to their section, equally loyal to the nation, open-minded and high-minded, who are eager to give the South a new policy, to rid it of sectionalism, to organize its spiritual, moral and intellectual forces, to develop education, and to treat great questions from a national rather than from a sectional point of view; men like Governor Aycock, of North Carolina, and Governor Montague, of Virginia. There is a whole group of educational leaders who represent the best of the Old South and the best of the New. It is the duty of wise, patriotic men in the North to cooperate with these new leaders; to strengthen their hands; to recognize and aid the best sentiment in the South, and to stimulate its activity. The Negro question can be settled by cooperation of the North with the South, by sympathy, by understanding; it can never be settled in any other way.

"What Gov. Aycock, of North Carolina, Thinks

"I am proud of my state because we have solved the Negro problem, which recently seems to have given you some trouble. We have taken him out of politics, and have thereby secured good government under any party, and laid foundations for the future development of both

EDWARD A. JOHNSON

races. We have secured peace and rendered prosperity a certainty. I am inclined to give you our solution of this problem. It is, first, as far as possible, under the Fifteenth Amendment, to disfranchise him; after that, let him alone; quit writing about him; quit talking about him; quit making him 'the white man's burden'; let him 'tote his own skillet'; quit coddling him; let him learn that no man, no race, ever got anything worth the having that he did not himself earn; that character is the outcome of sacrifice, and worth is the result of toil; that, whatever his future may be, the present has in it for him nothing that is not the product of industry, thrift, obedience to law and uprightness; that he cannot, by resolution of council or league, accomplish anything; that he can do much by work; that violence may gratify his passions, but it cannot accomplish his ambition; that he may rarely eat of the cooking equality, but he will always find when he does that there is death in the pot. Let the white man determine that no man shall by act or thought or speech cross this line, and the race problem will be at an end."

AFTER READING THESE THE DOCTOR explained that, about the time I left, the Negro population of the South began to drift towards the Northern states, where better wages were offered, on account of the improvements going on there.

"The farms were the first to be affected by this turn in affairs," said the Doctor. "In fact, the Negroes who had no land very generally left the farms and this so crippled the cotton industry that within ten years after the disfranchising acts were passed, there wasn't a 'ten horse' farm (to quote the expression used in the records) to be found in some of the Southern states for miles and miles. Every Negro laborer who went North found times so much better that he wrote back for his friends. The disfranchising acts seemed to give the disorderly element in Southern society a free hand. The result was that Negroes were mobbed with impunity for the slightest offences. In one instance I read of a Negro who accidentally stepped on a white man's foot. He was promptly knocked down. As it occurred in a public place where a small crowd had gathered to look at base-ball bulletins, seven or eight of the white by-standers in the crowd took a kick and a knock at him. A policeman appeared on the scene, who arrested the Negro and put him under lock and key—because he got knocked down!—as my father used to say in relating the story. Then, too, the newspapers continued to hold the Negro up to ridicule and whereas he formerly had some of his race on juries, they were now excluded.[10]

"You can imagine that it was getting very uncomfortable for the Negroes in the South about that time. Many of them left for the North and West. Quite a number went to Africa—and Bishop Smith of the African Methodist Church induced many to go to Hayti. Vast tracts of land in the Southwestern part of the United States were opened up to the cultivation of cotton by a national system of irrigation, and the Government employed Negroes on these improvements and also in the cultivation of the plant itself, after the irrigation system was perfected."

"What happened to the Southern white farmers?" I inquired.

"They moved to the cities in large numbers and engaged in manufacturing. As you will see when you begin to travel with me the South is now a great manufacturing country. This, they found later, was a mistake, as they lost race vitality and became virtually the slaves of the manufacturers, on whom they had to depend for bread from week to week. The National Government, however, came to the relief of the South in quite a substantial way (at the same time that it assumed control of all coal and iron mines, and oil wells) by buying up the cotton lands and parcelling them out to young Negroes at a small price, accompanied with means and assistance for the production of the crop. This was an act of the highest statesmanship and a great help in the solution of the Negro problem. It should have come immediately after reconstruction, but the intervening interests of political parties and ambitious men prevented it. A matter of serious moment for a long time was how to eliminate party and personal interests from the equation of politics. Too often good measures were opposed by the different political parties with

---

10. DOES THE NEGRO GET JUSTICE IN OUR COURTS?
(Charlotte, N. C., News.)

The Charlotte Observer makes the sweeping statement regarding the Negro: "He is not ill-treated nor improperly discriminated against except in the courts, and for the injustice done him there, there seems to be no remedy."

A CLOSE CONTEST.
(Charlotte, N. C., Observer.)

We always feel sorry for a North Carolina jury which gets hold of a case in which a black man is the plaintiff and the Southern Railway Company the defendant. A jury in Rowan superior court last week had such a case and must have been greatly perplexed about which party to the suit to decide against. After due deliberation, however, it decided—how do you suppose—Why, against the railroad. But the problem was one which called for fasting and prayer.

an eye singly to these interests. The great work of General O. O. Howard in connection with what was known as the Freedmen's Bureau was greatly hampered and met an untimely end because of the selfishness and partisanship of that period. In fact, this one feature has stood in the way of progress in this Government from its earliest existence. Example after example might be cited where party policy and personal interest has blocked the wheels of useful legislation.

"Oxenstiern said, 'See my son, with how little wisdom nations are governed.'

"It is wonderful how tolerant the people of the world have been in respect to bad government. No group of business men would have allowed its directors to spend the company's earnings in the way the rulers of the world have done from time immemorial. America has overlooked many of these points because of the unlimited opportunities here for money making—let the high tide of prosperity once ebb and then these defects become apparent! There were usually in a government office twice as many employed to do small tasks as any business organization would have thought of hiring, and they were paid excellent salaries. In other words, the more places a boss could fill with his constituents or friends, the more public money he could cause to be spent in his district, the more sinecures he could get for his constituents, the more popular he became. In addition to all this, he wasted the people's money with long speeches which were often printed and distributed at the Government's expense. The National Congress formerly was a most expensive institution. Its methods of business were highly extravagant and very often the time consumed resulted in accomplishing nothing more than a mere pittance, perhaps, of the work to be done; and that was carried through because of party advantage or personal interest."

V

A Visit to Public Buildings

The time had now arrived for our promised visit to some of the public buildings of the city and we seated ourselves in an electric motor car which the Doctor had summoned by touching a button. To my surprise, it made the trip alone, by traversing a course made for this purpose, somewhat on the order of the cash delivery systems formerly used in our large stores, being elevated some twenty feet above the surface. The coaches were arranged to come at a call from any number on certain streets.

The Doctor suggested that we should first visit the "Administration Building." I was expecting to find Congress or some such body in session, but to my surprise I was told by the Doctor that Congress had been abolished, and that the country was run on what I had formerly understood as the corporation plan; except that the salaries were not so large. The business of the Government was entrusted to bureaus or departments, and the officers in them were chosen for their fitness by an improved system of civil service.

"Who is president now," I inquired.

"President!" replied the Doctor, in surprise, "why we have none. I never saw a president. We need none. We have an Executive Department which fills his place."

"What as to proposing new measures?" I asked. "Who writes the annual messages suggesting them?"

"All this is left to a bureau chosen for that purpose, whose duties are to keep the nation informed as to its needs, and to formulate new plans, which are carried out along the idea of the *initiative* and *referendum* system with which you are doubtless somewhat acquainted, as I notice that it was discussed as early as 1890."

I replied that I had a recollection of seeing the terms but I could not give an intelligent definition of them. Whereupon the Doctor explained the system.

"You see," he said, "that the time wasted in Congressional debate is saved and the chance to block needed legislation is reduced to a minimum. There are no political offices to parcel out to henchmen, and the ambitions of demagogues are not fostered at the expense of the people. England, you will recollect, has had a king only in name for four hundred years. The American people have found out there is no necessity for either king, president, parliament or congress, and in that respect we may be able sooner or later to teach the mother country a lesson."

"To say I am surprised at all this, Dr. Newell, is to express my feelings but mildly," said I, "but I can now see how the changes in reference to the Negro have been brought about. Under our political system, such as I knew it to be, these results could not have been reached in a thousand years!"

"Yes, Mr. Twitchell," replied the Doctor, "our new system, as it may be called, has been a great help in settling, not only the Negro problem, but many others; for instance the labor question, about which we have already conversed,—and the end is not yet, the hey-day of our glory is not reached and will not be until the principles of the Golden Rule have become an actuality in this land."

I here remarked that I always felt a misgiving as to our old system, which left the Government and management of the people's affairs in the hands of politicians who had more personal interest than statesmanship; but I could not conceive of any method of ridding the country of this influence and power, and had about resolved to accept the situation as a part of my common lot with humanity.

Doctor Newell stated that there was much opposition to the parcelling out of land to Negro farmers. It was jeered at as "paternalism," and "socialistic," and "creating a bad precedent."

"But," said he, "our Bureau of Public Utility carried out the idea with the final endorsement of the people, who now appreciate the wisdom of the experiment. The government could as well afford to spend public money for the purpose of mitigating the results of race feeling as it could to improve rivers and harbors. In both instances the public good was served. If bad harbors were a curse so was public prejudice on the race question. It was cheaper in the long run to remove the cause than to patch up with palliatives. If the Negro was becoming vicious to a large extent, and the cause of it was the intensity of race prejudice in the land, which confined him to menial callings, and only a limited number of those; and race prejudice could not be well prevented owing to the misconception of things by those who fostered it; and if an attempt at suppression would mean more bitterness toward the Negro and danger to the country, then surely, looking at the question from the distance at which we are today, the best solution was the one adopted by our bureaus at the time. At least, we know the plan was successful, and 'nothing succeeds like success!'

"I am inclined to the opinion that the politicians, judging by the magazine article I gave you," said he, "were quite anxious to keep the Negro question alive for the party advantage it brought. In the North it served the purpose of solidifying the Negro vote for the Republicans, and in the South the Democrats used it to their advantage; neither party, therefore, was willing to remove the Negro issue by any real substantial legislation. Enough legislation was generally proposed *pro* and *con* to excite the voters desired to be reached, and there the efforts ended."

I could not but reflect that the triumph of reason over partisanship and demagoguery had at last been reached, and that the American people had resolved no longer to temporize with measures or men, but were determined to have the government run according to the original design of its founders, upon the principle of the greatest good to the greatest number.

No President since Grant was ever more abused by a certain class of newspapers and politicians than President Roosevelt, who adopted the policy of appointing worthy men to office, regardless of color. He said that fitness should be his rule and not color. In his efforts to carry out this policy he met with the most stubborn resistance from those politicians who hoped to make political capital out of the Negro question. To his credit let it be said that he refused to bow the knee to Baal but stood by his convictions to the end.

I found from the published reports of the Bureau of Statistics that the Negro's progress in one hundred years had been all that his friends could have hoped for. I give below a comparative table showing the difference:

	A.D. 1900	A.D. 2004
Aggregate Negro Wealth	$890,000,000	$2,670,000,000
Aggregate Negro population	8,840,789	21,907,079
Per cent. of illiteracy	45 per cent.	2 per cent.
Per cent. of crime	20 per cent.	1 per cent.
Ratio of home owners	1 in 100	1 in 30.
Ratio of insane	1 in 1000	1 in 500.
Death rate	20 per M.	5 per M.

Number of lawyers	250	5,282
Number of doctors	800	11,823
Number of pharmacists	150	2,111
Number of teachers	30,000	200,603
Number of preachers	75,000	250,804
Number of mechanics	80,000	240,922

I noticed that Negroes had gained standing in the country as citizens and were no longer objects for such protection as the whites thought a Negro deserved. They stood on the same footing legally as other people. It was a pet phrase in my time for certain communities to say to the Negro that they "would protect him in his rights," but what the Negro wanted was that he should not have to be protected at all! He wanted public sentiment to protect him just as it did a white man. This proffered help was all very good, since it was the best the times afforded, but it made the Negro's rights depend upon what his white neighbors said of him,—if these neighbors did not like him his rights were *nil*. His was an ephemeral existence dependent on the whims and caprices of friends or foes. True citizenship must be deeper than that and be measured by the law of the land—not by the opinion of one's neighbors.

But the voice of the politician who wished to contort civil into social equality was now hushed. He no more disgraced the land, and a Negro could have a business talk with a white man on the street of a Southern city without either party becoming subjects of criticism for practicing "social equality."

VI

A Ride with Irene

S oon after this talk Miss Davis and I visited prominent places in the city of Phœnix. I had anxiously waited for this opportunity. An uncontrollable desire to fulfill this engagement had grown on me, from the day she informed me that she had planned the outing. We visited McPherson's monument, and standing with head uncovered in its shadow, I said that I was glad to see that the cause he fought for was recognized as a blessing to the South as well as to the North. She replied that some of her relatives perished in defense of the South, but she had been often told by her father that her ancestors considered slavery a great wrong and liberated their slaves by will.

"In fact," she remarked with womanly intuition, "I can see no reason for their having had slaves at the outset. Why couldn't the Negroes have served us, from the first, as *freemen*, just as they did after their emancipation? What was the necessity for adopting a system that gave a chance for the brutal passions of bad men to vent themselves? The whole country has suffered in its moral tone because of slavery, and we are not as pure minded a nation today as we should have been without it."

I replied that it was commercialism that fixed slavery in the nation and rooted and grounded it so deep that scarcely could it be eradicated without destroying the nation itself. I noticed that she had none of the Southern woman's prejudice against "Yankees," so prevalent in my day, and that she was far enough removed from the events of the Civil War to look at them dispassionately.

What a difference doth time make in people and nations. What is wisdom today may be the grossest folly tomorrow, and the popular theme of today maybe ridiculed later on. Ye "men of the hour" beware! The much despised Yankee has taught the South many lessons in industry, in the arts, sciences and literature, but none more valuable to her than to forsake her prejudice against the evolution of the Negro.

We rode out to Chattahoochee farm, noted for its picturesqueness and "up-to-dateness," a paying institution entirely under the management of Negroes. The superintendent was a graduate from the State Agricultural College for Negroes, near Savannah.

"Are there any other farms of this kind in the state under Negro management," I asked.

She replied that there were many, that a majority of the landowners of the state had found it profitable to turn vast tracts of land over to these young Negro graduates, who were proving themselves adepts in the art of scientific farming, making excellent salaries, and returning good dividends on the investments.

I remarked that I used to wonder why this could not be done with the young Negroes coming out from such schools—since their ante-bellum fathers were so successful in this line—and I further said that this movement might have been inaugurated in my day, but for the opposition of the politicians, who approached the Negro question generally with no sincere desire to get effective results, but to make political capital for themselves.

She at once suggested, "And so you believe it was a good idea then to dispense with the politicians?"

"Indeed," said I, "they were horrible stumps in the road of progress."

We ended our ride after a visit to the park, which was a beautiful spot. It served not only as a place of recreation, but Musical, Zoölogical, Botanical and Aquarian departments were open to the public, and free lectures were given on the latest inventions and improvements, thus coupling information with recreation, and elevating the thoughts and ideas of the people. I noticed the absence of the old time signs which I had heard once decorated the gates of this park, "Negroes and dogs not allowed." Of course Irene had never seen or heard of such a thing and I therefore did not mention my thoughts to her. She was a creature of the new era and knew the past only from books and tradition. I had the misfortune, or pleasure, as the case may be, of having lived in two ages and incidents of the past would continually rise before me in comparison with the present.

On reaching my room that evening I felt that my trip with Miss Davis had been very agreeable and very instructive, but still there was an aching void—for what I did not know. Was it that we did not converse on some desired subject?

VII

Dr. Newell and Work of the Young Ladies' Guilds

These Guilds," said Dr. Newell, taking my arm as we left the dinner table one afternoon, "are most excellent institutions. Nothing has done more to facilitate a happy solution of the so-called Negro problem of the past than they, and their history is a most fascinating story, as it pictures their origin by a a young Southern heroine of wealth and standing with philanthropic motives, who while on her way to church one Sunday morning was moved by the sight of a couple of barefooted Negro children playing in the street. Her heart went out to them. She thought of the efforts being made for the heathen abroad, when the needy at our very doors were neglected. Moved towards the work as if by inspiration, she gave her whole time and attention and considerable of her vast wealth to organizing these guilds all over the country. She met with much opposition and was ridiculed as the 'nigger angel,' but this did not deter her and she lived to see the work she organized planted and growing in all the Southland. Cecelia was her name and the incorporated name of these organizations is the Cecilian Guild."

"I should be glad to read the history of this movement," said I, "for all I have learned about it through Miss Davis and yourself is exceedingly interesting."

"One of the problems met with in the outset was that of the fallen woman," said the Doctor, "although the Negroes were never so immoral as was alleged of them. You will recall that after the Civil War many of the slave marriages were declared illegal and remarriage became necessary. Twenty-five cents was the license fee. Thousands showed their faithfulness to each other by complying with this law—a most emphatic argument of the Negro's faithfulness to the marriage vows. Day after day long files of these sons of Africa stood in line waiting with their 'quarters' in hand to renew their vows to the wife of their youth. Many were old and infirm—a number were young and vigorous, there was no compulsion and the former relations might have been severed and other selections made; but not so, they were renewing the old vows and making legal in freedom that which was illegal now because of slavery. Would the 500,000 white divorcees in America in your time have done this?" the doctor asked.

"Let me relate to you a story connected with the work of one of the Cecilian Guilds," said the doctor. "A bright faced octoroon girl living in one of our best Southern homes became peculiarly attractive to a brother of her mistress, a young woman of much character, who loved her maid and loved her brother. The situation grew acute; heroic treatment became necessary as the octoroon related to her mistress in great distress every approach and insinuation made by the young Lothario, his avowals of love, his promises to die for her, his readiness to renounce all conventionalities and flee with her to another state. To all this the octoroon was like ice. Her mother had been trained in the same household and was honored and beloved. Her father was an octoroon— and the girl was a chip of both old blocks. The mistress remonstrated, threatened and begged her brother to no avail, and finally decided to send the girl North, as a last resort, a decision which pleased the maid, who desired to be rid of her tormentor.

"But the trip North only made matters worse. Two years after Eva had made her home with a family in Connecticut, John Guilford turns up. He had been married to his cousin, whom he didn't love, and while practising medicine in one of the leading cities had become distinguished in his profession. He met Eva during a professional visit to her new home in Connecticut. The old flame was rekindled. He concealed the fact of his marriage and offered her his hand, stating that he must take her to another town and keep her incognito, to avoid ruining his practice by the gossip which his marriage to a servant girl would naturally create. Fair promises—which generally do 'butter parsnips,' in love affairs, at least—overcame the fair Eva; she consented to marry the young physician. She lived in another town, she bore him children, he loved her. Finally the real wife, who had borne him no offspring, ascertained the truth. Her husband pleaded hard with her, told her of his love for the girl and how, under the spell of his fondness for children, and following the example of the great Zola, he had yielded to the tempter. 'But,' he begged, 'forgive me because of your love—save my name and our fortune.' This she finally did. Poor Eva, when her second child was four years old, died, never knowing but that she was the true wife of her deceiver. Her children were adopted by the Guilfords as their own, grew up and entered society under the Guilford name and no one today will charge them with their father's sin."

VIII

WITH IRENE AGAIN

I frequently saw Irene during the few weeks of my sojourn at the Newell residence, but hers was a busy life and there was not much time for *tête-à-tête*. One evening, however, she seated herself by my side on the veranda and amid the fragrance of the flowers and the songs of the birds we had an hour alone which passed so swiftly that it seemed but a moment. Time hangs heavy only on the hands of those who are not enjoying it. I had noticed her anxiety for a letter and her evident disappointment in the morning when the pneumatic tube in the Newell residence did not deliver it.

Not purposely, but unavoidably, I saw a few days later an envelope postmarked, "Philippines." I ventured to say, with an attempt at teasing, that I trusted she was in good humor today since her letter had come, and surmised that it bore "a message of friendship or love" for her. She adroitly avoided the subject, which was all the evidence I wanted to assure me of the truth of my theory as to its contents. The clue was given which I intended to establish in asking the question. Love may be blind but it has ways for trailing its game.

Finding no encouragement for pursuing this subject further, I turned to the discussion of books and finally asked if she had read an old book which in my day used to be referred to as, "Tom Dixon's Leopard's Spots." She said she had not, but had seen it instanced as a good example of that class of writers who misrepresented the best Southern sentiment and opinion. She stated that her information was that there was not a godly character in the book, that it represented the Southern people as justifying prejudice, and ill treatment of a weaker race, whose faults were admittedly forgivable by reason of circumstances. She also stated that "the culture of the present time places such writers in the same class with that English Lord who once predicted that a steamer could never cross the Atlantic for the reason that she could never carry enough fuel to make the voyage."

"And probably in such cases the wish was father to the thought," I added.

She also had heard of those false prophets whom history had not forgotten, but who lived only in ridicule and as examples of error. She seemed to be ashamed of the ideas once advocated by these men, and charitably dismissed them with the remark that, "It would have been better for the cause of true Christianity had they never been listened to by so large a number of our people, as they represented brute force rather than the Golden Rule."

I heard with rapt attention. Although I had already seen much to convince me of the evolution of sentiment in the South, these words sank deeper than all else. Here was a woman of aristocratic Southern blood, cradled under the hills of secession and yet vehement in denunciation of those whom I had learned to recognize as the beacon lights of Southern thought and purpose! And when I reflected that her views were then the views of the whole South, I indeed began to realize the wonderful transformation I was being permitted to see. I silently prayed, "God bless the New South!" My heart was full, I felt that I had met a soul that was a counterpart of my own,—"Each heart shall seek its kindred heart, and cling to it, as close as ever."

The pent-up feelings of my breast must find some expression of admiration for her lofty ideals of joy, for the triumph I had been permitted to see of truth over error in the subjugation of America's greatest curse, *prejudice*, and finally of the meeting with a congenial spirit in flesh and blood, and of the opposite sex; which alone creates for man a halo peculiarly its own.

I was hardly myself, and I burst forth with, "Irene, are you engaged to the man in the 'Philippines'?"

I was rather presumptuous, but the gentle reply was, "I will tell you some other time"—and we parted.

IX

The Prize Essay

In looking for the cause of so many improvements I found that the Bureau of Public Utility had been of great service to the country in bringing about such a happy solution of the Negro problem. Among other novel methods adopted I found they had established public boarding schools. I was astonished to learn that they were based on some suggestions made by a Negro of my own times, in an essay which had won a prize of $100 offered by a Northern philanthropist. The writer was a Southern Negro from the state of North Carolina. His ideas were carried out in a general scheme of education for the Negro.

The good results of this course have proved their wisdom; in fact the results were of such importance as to warrant my reproducing part of what he wrote:

The Kind of Education The Negro Needs

"I have noticed a growing tendency in the writings of those whites who discuss the racial question, in the newspapers, towards helpfulness and kindness to the Negro race. Some articles are very bitter, abusive, and unfair, the writers seeming to be either playing to the galleries of a maudlin sentiment or venting personal spleen—but in the main this is not so. The Negroes, who withal had rather love than hate white people, are generally thankful for all expressions favorable to themselves. They realize as a mass that there has grown up within the last thirty years an idle, vicious class of Negroes whose acts and habits are of such a nature as to make them objectionable to their own race, as well as to the whites. What to do with this class is a problem that perplexes the better element of Negroes, more, possibly, than it does the whites; since their shortcomings are generally credited to the whole Negro race, which is wrong as a fact and unjust in theory.

"This vicious element in the race is a constant subject of discussion in Negro churches and in private conversation. It is a mistake to say that crime is not condemned by the better class of Negroes. There may be a class that attend the courts when their 'pals' are in jeopardy and who rejoice to see them exonerated, but the real substantial Negro man is seldom seen 'warming the benches' of court rooms. Unlike the white spectators, who are men of leisure and spend their time there out of interest in what is going on, and often to earn a *per diem* as jurors,—the leisure class in the Negro race is generally composed of those who have 'served time' in prison or of their associates.

"The Negro problem, as now considered, seems, so far as the discussion of it is concerned, to be entirely in the hands of white people for solution, and the Negro himself is supposed to have no part in it, other than to 'wait and tend' on the bidding of those engaged at the job. He is 'a looker on in Venice.' I therefore offer my suggestion as to method or plan with fear of being asked to stand aside. Yet, in my zeal for the work and in my anxiety to have it accomplished as speedily and correctly as possible, I venture a few suggestions, the result of twenty years' observation and experience in teaching, which appear to my mind as the best way to go at this Herculean task.

"In the first place I suggest that the boarding school is the only one fitted for the final needs of the young of the race—a school where culture and civility would be taught hand in hand with labor and letters. The main object in education is training for usefulness. 'Leading out' is the meaning of the term education, and what the young of the race needs is to be lead out, and kept out of vice, until the danger period is passed. The public schools turn out the child just at that period when temptations are most alluring. From the age of puberty to twenty-one is the danger time, and the time of forming character. The kind of character then formed remains. If the child can be steered over this period, under right influences and associations, the problem of his future is comparatively settled for good, otherwise for bad. Too much is expected of the public schools as now constituted, if it is presumed that they can mould both the mind and the heart of the child; when they usually drop him just at the period that he begins to learn he has a heart and a mind! He is mostly an animal during the period allotted to him in the public schools. Many are fortunate enough to have parents who have the leisure and ability to train them properly. Some follow up the course in the public schools with a season in a boarding school—these are fortunate, but where is the great mass? They became boot-blacks, runaways, 'dudes,' or temporary domestics, in which calling they earn money more to satisfy their youthful propensities than for any settled purpose for the future of their lives.

"Out of six hundred pupils who had left one public school in Virginia I found only 85 who had settled down with any seemingly fixed purpose. I counted 196 who had become domestics, and, either married or single, are making orderly citizens. The rest have become mere bilge water and are unknown. Among the girls fourteen are of the *demirep* order. The public schools are doing some work it is true—a great work, all things considered—but their 'reach' is not far enough. What the young of the Negro race needs, beyond all things, is training—not only of the head, but of the heart and hand as well. The boarding school would meet the requirements, if properly conducted. The girl and boy should remain at useful employment under refined influences until the habit of doing things right and acting right is formed. How can the public schools mould character in a child whom they have for five hours, while the street gamins have him for the rest of the day? And further, as before stated, when the child leaves the public schools at the time when most of all he is likely to get into bad habits?

"Good home training is the salvation of any people. Many Negro children are necessarily lacking in this respect, for the reason that their parents are called off to their places of labor during the day and the children are left to shift for themselves. Too often when the parents are at home the influence is not of the most wholesome, thus there is a double necessity for the inauguration of a system of training that will eliminate this evil. The majority of working people do not earn sufficient wages to hire governesses for their children,—if they should quit work and attempt the task for themselves the children would suffer for bread, and soon the state would be called upon to support them as paupers. The state is unable in the present condition of public sentiment to pass upon the sufficiency of wages from employer to employee, but it *can* dictate the policy of the school system. All selfish or partisan scruples should be eliminated and the subject should be approached with wisdom and foresight, looking solely to accomplishing the best results possible.

"My idea is to supplement the term of the public schools, which might be reduced to four years, by a three years' term in a public boarding school in which the pupil could do all the work and produce enough in vacation to make the school self-sustaining; except the item of the salaries of the teachers, who would be employed by the state. Make three years in these schools compulsory on all who are not able to or do not, select a school of their own choice. Three years' military service is demanded of the adults in most of the European states, which is time almost thrown away so far as the individual is concerned, but a three years' service in schools of this kind would be of the greatest advantage of the child and state as well.

"*How it can be done*
"There is idle land enough to be used for the establishment of such schools in every township in the South, and with the proper training in them, the pupils from such institutions would come out and build up hundreds of places that are now going to waste for lack of attention. The solution of the race problem cannot be effected by talk alone, nor by a reckless expenditure of public funds, but if the state is to undertake the education of its children with good citizenship in view—thus becoming as it were the *parens patriæ*, then let the job be undertaken as a parent would be likely to go at it for his own children. In well regulated communities wayward children are placed in homes which the wisdom of experience has found to be the best place for them, and they come out useful citizens. If the youth of the colored race is incorrigible because of instinct or environment, or both, the place for them is in some kind of home where they can be protected

against themselves and society, and trained and developed. Let them have four years of training in the public schools and emerge from these into 'a boarding and working school.' This would be far better than furnishing a chain gang system for them to go into after bad character has been formed.

"'An ounce of prevention is worth a pound of cure' right here, and is a cheaper and a more substantial investment. Experience shows that the vicious become *more vicious* by confinement in the chain gangs, and it not infrequently happens that individuals, after having been degraded by a first sentence, become outcasts and spend from a half to two-thirds of their lives thereafter in prison. The chain gang system can hardly be urged in any sense as a reformatory, and from the frequent returns thereto of the criminal class can be hardly styled as a first-class preventive of crime. It is simply an institution in which criminals can be kept out of their usual occupations. While they are so confined crime is that much decreased, but it opens up again on their exit.

"The value of the boarding school idea as a supplement to the public school system is borne out by the statistics of the boarding schools already established for colored people by private funds. The pupils turned out by these schools are a credit to the race and the state. They are good citizens, they accumulate property, they are industrious and upright. There is not one case in a thousand where you find them on the court records. They are the genuine 'salt of the earth,' so far as the product of the schools for the freedmen is concerned. The public schools have been the feeders in a large measure of these private schools, but only a small percentage of those who leave the public schools ever reach private schools. Under the plan above suggested all pupils will spend three years in a private school, or a school of that nature which will accomplish the same end.

"If the Negro has a greater native tendency to crime than the other races, as is urged by some, then it is necessary to take more care in protecting him against it. If his disease is of a more malignant type than ordinary when it attacks him, then the more heroic should be the remedy. It is as illogical to apply a system of education to a child who is not prepared for it as it would be to treat a patient for appendicitis when he has the eczema. *Results* are what the state wants, and if the schools now established are not giving them, the system should be changed to one that for thirty years has been a success. The money sent South by Northern charity has not been wasted. Some people think it has destroyed some farm hands—this may be true, but it has created larger producers in other lines fully as beneficial to the state as farming.

"The state is suffering because of its criminal class both white and black, and it will continue to do so until this cloud is removed, and in undertaking the education of its citizens, the state is not working for the farmers especially (as some seem to imply by their arguments on this subject) but for a higher type of citizenship along *all* lines. 'More intelligence in farming, mining, manufacturing, and business' is the motto, a general uplift in which all shall be benefited. Neither the farmer, the miner nor the manufacturer can hope to build up a serf class for his special benefit. The state has not established the school system for that purpose, and should the theory once obtain that it was so established, the handwriting would at once appear on the wall. The ideal school system is that in which each citizen claims his part with all the rest. No line should be drawn in the division of the funds to the schools, and as a fit corollary to this, they should not be established to foster the financial interests of any one class of citizens as against another. *Pro bono publico* is their motto and may it ever remain so!"

I MIGHT ADD THAT AS a substantial proof of the great success of the new system of Negro education the Southern states have joined in preparing a great Negro Exposition, open to Negroes all over the world, in which, it is expected, a fine showing will be made by members of the race in almost every field of human endeavor.

X

Sad News for Irene

Two years have passed since Irene promised, on the veranda of the Newell residence, to tell Gilbert Twitchell if her hand was pledged to the man in the Philippines from whom she had received a letter. Other and sadder news had come since that time. The young officer (Kennesaw Malvern) was dead. He was accidentally shot during a target practice on a U. S. vessel cruising in the Philippines, where by the way peace and independence have long prevailed. Irene was now in black for him. She saw Gilbert Twitchell not quite so often as before, but her mourning robes made it unnecessary that she should answer the question he propounded to her on the veranda.

At the first opportunity, however, Gilbert told her that he loved her, but that he would not ask her hand in marriage till such a time as she thought proper. Her reply was that her whole soul was a complete wreck. She felt as if the world had no further charm, and that death would be welcome if she knew she would be with *him*.

But time works many changes, even in such a constant and abiding force as a true woman's love. God made them sincere, it may be said, but few there are that stand the test of time, and the assaults of a persistent man's devotion. Many would freeze their hearts if they could, but the manly temperature is too high in most cases and they melt sooner or later under its radiations. Sometimes in her despair, in her dilemma, in her war between the heart force and the will, she resolves to marry her beseecher "to be rid of him," too considerate of his feelings to say "no," and too true to former pledges to say "yes." What tunes indeed may "mere man" play on such heart-strings!

All this was not the case with Irene exactly, but it was true in some particulars, for Irene was a *woman*, and the only important truth to Gilbert was that the year 2007 saw them husband and wife and that the love that once went to the Philippines was bestowed on the man she helped rescue from his trip in an air ship.

A Note About the Author

Edward A. Johnson (1860–1944) was an African American attorney, novelist, and New York state assemblyman. Born into slavery in Wake County, North Carolina, he gained his freedom as a child at the end of the Civil War and went on to excel at Washington High School and Atlanta University. While working as a school principal in Raleigh, he wrote *A School History of the Negro Race in America from 1619 to 1890* (1890), a pioneering textbook on African American history that was adopted by black schools throughout Virginia and North Carolina. In 1891, he obtained a law degree from Shaw University, a historically black university in Raleigh, before working as an assistant U.S. Attorney from 1899 to 1907. During this time, Johnson wrote *Light Ahead for the Negro* (1904) an influential utopian novel set in the year 2006. Devoted to Republican Party politics, he moved to New York City and became a leader in Harlem, eventually joining the New York State Assembly in 1918. In 1928, despite having gone blind several years earlier, Johnson ran a strong campaign for Congress in the 21st District, eventually losing to Democrat Royal H. Weller.

A Note from the Publisher

Spanning many genres, from non-fiction essays to literature classics to children's books and lyric poetry, Mint Edition books showcase the master works of our time in a modern new package. The text is freshly typeset, is clean and easy to read, and features a new note about the author in each volume. Many books also include exclusive new introductory material. Every book boasts a striking new cover, which makes it as appropriate for collecting as it is for gift giving. Mint Edition books are only printed when a reader orders them, so natural resources are not wasted. We're proud that our books are never manufactured in excess and exist only in the exact quantity they need to be read and enjoyed.

bookfinity™

Discover more of your favorite classics with Bookfinity™.

- Track your reading with custom book lists.
- Get great book recommendations for your personalized Reader Type.
- Add reviews for your favorite books.
- AND MUCH MORE!

Visit **bookfinity.com** and take the fun Reader Type quiz to get started.

Enjoy our classic and modern companion pairings!

Classic & Modern

Bookfinity is a registered trademark of Ingram Book Group LLC. © 2023 Bookfinity. All rights reserved.

Printed in the USA
CPSIA information can be obtained
at www.ICGtesting.com
JSHW021458170424
61355JS00004B/334